FALLING LEAVES

When Richard employs Annie to update the computer system for his company, she finds herself, through circumstance, living in his house. Although they are attracted to each other, Richard's daughter, Katie, takes a dislike to her. Added to this, Annie suspects that Richard is in love with someone else, so she allows herself to be drawn to Steve, Richard's accountant. Annie feels she must choose between love and a career — how can the complications in her life be resolved . . . ?

SHEILA BENTON

FALLING LEAVES

Complete and Unabridged

LINFORD
Leicester

First published in Great Britain in 2009

First Linford Edition
published 2010

British Library CIP Data

Benton, Sheila.
    Falling leaves. - - (Linford romance library)
    1. Computer technicians- -Fiction.
    2. Businessmen- -Fiction. 3. Love stories.
    4. Large type books.
    I. Title II. Series
    823.9'2–dc22

    ISBN 978–1–44480–180–4

Published by
F. A. Thorpe (Publishing)
Anstey, Leicestershire

Set by Words & Graphics Ltd.
Anstey, Leicestershire
Printed and bound in Great Britain by
T. J. International Ltd., Padstow, Cornwall

This book is printed on acid-free paper

For my husband

1

The ringing of the telephone broke the heavy silence and, keeping her fingers crossed that it might be work, Annie reached for the receiver. 'Hi Annie, can you help us out with a job?'

'Jo,' she recognised the voice of her ex colleague. 'You must be my fairy godmother, I've got absolutely nothing on at the moment.'

'Brilliant, because someone is on his way who needs help. It's nothing too drastic, just alterations to a job we did in the New Forest.

'New Forest?'

'Yes, it'll mean staying there for a short while.'

'Okay,' Annie laughed. 'I don't care where it is as long as it's work.'

'Em . . . ' Jo hesitated. 'There's just one thing I want to mention. I'm told this client is a great guy when you get to know him but on first impression he can be very off-hand.'

'Right, I'll consider myself warned.'

'Just don't let him intimidate you or you'll get off to a bad start.'

'Okay, no problem and thanks a lot for the call.'

She remembered her friend's warning when she heard the brisk knock at her office door that sounded both confident and impatient. Strangely enough those two words summed up the man who reached the front of her desk in a single stride.

Instantly she was on her guard, knowing that here was someone who was used to getting what he wanted.

'Annie Ashley?' he rapped out as though just asking for her name was wasting his precious time.

'Yes.' There was something about the sheer power of him that made her feel defensive, causing her to make her voice as firm as she could manage.

'Well, is she in?'

'Em . . . actually I'm Annie Ashley.'

Hell, she thought, why am I stuttering and stumbling? Squaring her shoulders she stood up and held out her hand.

His eyes narrowed. 'You look very young.' A searching grey gaze ran over her, noting the dark blonde hair and thickly lashed blue eyes.

Her hand was hanging in mid air and she was about to withdraw it when his arm shot out and grasped her fingers in a grip that almost hurt.

Taking her time she repeated his observation, 'Yes I do look young.' Then she laughed and added, 'but as time goes on it can only be an advantage.' There was something about him that made her defensive.

Her eyes looked up a long way to meet his cold grey stare. He'd be good looking if he weren't so impatient, she mused.

'Won't you take a seat?' She pointed to the other chair in the room. This man was far too large to argue with while he was standing up.

Pulling the chair closer and sitting

down, he looked at his watch as though he grudged every moment. Even sitting down he dwarfed the tiny office that was her new pride and joy.

Clearing her throat slightly, she knew that it was going to be difficult. This man, who must be well over six foot, had aggression shouting from every inch of his broad-shouldered frame. She frowned, noting that although he was expensively dressed, the dark business suit was somehow at odds with his healthy outdoor complexion and the sun streaks in the front of his hair. Here was someone who spent a great deal of his time in the open and she wondered idly what he did to maintain that tan. Quickly bringing her mind back from its meanderings she started to speak.

'Perhaps you'd like to introduce yourself.' She looked at him knowing he was a prospective client and business was thin but remembering her friend's words she was determined not to be intimidated by him.

4

He glanced around the room as though expecting someone else to appear. 'I'm sorry,' he said abruptly. 'I'm Richard Ellis and you must think me rather bad mannered.'

She raised her eyebrows slightly just so that he would know she agreed with every word he said.

'The point is I've taken a day off from my own business to come here. Well, not straight here exactly, I've been to Galling Computer Software.'

Annie nodded as she thought fondly about her first job; Gallings had trained her well enough to start her own consultancy, and were even now passing her work, which she desperately needed in these difficult times. In fact without them she'd be struggling.

'They designed my original computer package and I want some alterations done quickly.' He frowned, looked steadily at her as though making sure she was listening properly. 'Unfortunately they are overloaded themselves and referred me to you.'

'I used to work for them and they often pass me jobs.'

His expression changed. 'I'm sorry but, as I said before I expected someone older.' He attempted a grin. 'It must be your name, 'Annie', it made me feel you were older. I've an elderly aunt with the same name.'

An image of an elderly aunt flashed into her mind and she stifled a giggle.

He must have caught her expression and said impatiently 'Can you do the job? I must have an immediate answer.'

Pushing back her chair with a determined scrape she stood to face him. 'Certainly I can do the job.' She held his stare. 'But you know that, or you wouldn't be here as Gallings have obviously recommended me.'

There was a long silence while they held each other's gaze like two fighters squaring up for another round. 'Well, if you really are as good as they say . . . ' It seemed that he had come to a decision and looked around the small office. 'Where can we talk?'

'Where?' She queried, her expression puzzled.

'Yes, where?'

Once more Annie concentrated on keeping her temper which was no easy task. She couldn't even indulge in counting to ten again as impatience radiated from him. 'Here of course,' she stuck her chin in the air, 'where else?' She hesitated and continued with more authority, 'In my office.'

'The whole of it, just this pocket sized space?' He raised his eyebrows. 'It's an overgrown broom cupboard.'

Hearing the amusement in his voice her breath caught in her throat and suddenly all the effort she had put into starting on her own seemed at risk and she rushed to the defence of her premises.

'You may not have noticed when you came in that this is a complex of small office units.' He made no reply and suddenly she saw everything through his eyes and knew that it was not impressive.

'Everyone here is running a new

enterprise of some sort that doesn't call for a lot of staff,' she rushed on, 'I have my own consultancy business and next door is Mark who is an accountant.' The words dried up as she had the distinct impression that he was silently laughing at her.

'You seem worried about my age but we all have to start somewhere,' she tried to sound more friendly once again eying his well tailored suit. After all she was gazing at the best specimen of manhood she'd seen in ages. His big rangy frame looked superbly fit with not a spare inch of flesh anywhere. And as he turned his head in the light from the window she couldn't see one grey strand amongst his casually styled fair hair. Superbly fit and incredibly attractive would describe him aptly she decided.

There was an edge to his voice 'Frankly, Miss Ashley I would prefer someone older.'

Anger bubbled up inside her at his arrogance.

'Maybe I'm not what you'd like but that doesn't mean that I can't do the job. I'm damned good at what I do.'

His mouth thinned. 'I've built up a business from just one shop my father used to own.' He paused and spoke slowly. 'A very successful business.'

'And I promise you I will be able to do the job,' she said firmly.

Surprisingly a swift look of admiration flashed across his face and he sank back into his chair. 'You've got plenty of spirit for a girl of your age. I admire that.'

A warm feeling crept upwards from somewhere deep inside and she was ridiculously pleased that he admired something about her. Standing there in front of him she realised the interview had got out of hand and, trying to put it back onto a different footing, she snapped more briskly than she intended. 'Let's get on to business then, shall we?'

The admiring look abruptly disappeared and opening his briefcase he spread a variety of papers over her desk, pausing fractionally to watch while she seated herself opposite him.

'This is what I want done.' He stated his instructions quickly, occasionally stopping while he thrust a paper under her nose or underlined something that was particularly important. The under-lining was done in a thick, black hand, very swift and very definite. Everything about him was quick and energetic and she only hoped she could keep up the pace. Willing herself to listen carefully she tried to absorb all that he said. At last it was over and he sat back, stretching out his legs, and looked at her.

For a moment there was silence then she forgot everything but the total involvement in her subject and was shooting questions at him and the answers were coming back quick as bullets. This was a discussion of equals where, if anything, Annie had the upper hand and looking up she saw a gradual respect in his eyes.

'Right,' he sat back, 'it seems that you understand what I need. How long will it take you to put it into operation? The quicker the better. I take it you've nothing at the moment that you can't leave?'

Momentarily she was tempted to invent something that needed her attention for the next few days and then shook her head. It was no use pretending that she was inundated with work; now was the time to be realistic. 'No, nothing. I can come right away.'

'Good and how long before I get results and what equipment will you need to get started?'

Her answer was ready. 'I'll need a computer to myself where I can design and work on the things you need, then I'll copy your existing data on to my own machine where I can work on the alterations without upsetting or inter-fering with the normal day to day running of your office. Once I've made and tested the alterations there will be a bit of disruption while I transfer the existing system on to the new and then . . . '

'I take it you'll stay and see it running smoothly,' he interrupted.

'Which was what I was about to say.'

'Sorry,' he had the grace to look ashamed. 'I apologise. I should warn you that I do tend to interrupt, patience is not my strong point.'

'I had noticed.'

'Time is money.'

'I understand. It's the same for everyone I work for so you're no different.' Oh goodness, she thought, if she didn't watch her tongue she'd end up as rude as him. He certainly brought out the worst in her.

'Your fee . . . ' He hesitated and then named a figure she knew would solve most of her financial worries.

'Quite acceptable,' she managed to say, hoping that surprise and relief wasn't showing on her face.

She looked across at him and saw that although his eyes were amused he was not smiling and then she realised he hadn't smiled once in all the time he'd been here. Not even in greeting. How could she work with a man who never smiled? Then gradually the corners of his mouth moved very slightly and she watched mesmerised as they twitched even more and suddenly there was a display of even teeth and he actually smiled.

Annie clutched the corner of her desk. This man was devastating when he smiled perhaps it was as well he didn't do it very often or she would have a hard time concentrating on the job in hand. Trying to drag her eyes away from his lips she noticed the tiny cleft in his chin. It was better to keep him in a mood, she decided or he would be dangerous in quite another way. Already she was feeling flushed and warm when she should be cool and efficient. She looked down at her desk and missed the expression in his eyes as he watched the colour run up to her cheeks.

Dimly aware that he had been

speaking she said, 'I beg your pardon?'

'I said, tomorrow then. I'll expect you about lunch time.'

'Tomorrow, but . . . ' She hesitated, not wanting to appear too available.

'You said you could come immediately.'

'Well, yes but . . . '

'Can you or can't you come immediately?' he said impatiently.

'Well, yes but I have things I need to arrange here.'

'You're not exactly inundated with work by the look of things.' He glanced swiftly round the room.

'I'm able to organise myself,' she said quickly before he spoke again.

'Do you drive or will you come on the train?'

'I'll drive but I'll need accommodation and . . . '

'I'll arrange it, all you have to do is just get there,' he shoved a card into her hands. 'Do you want directions?'

'No, no,' she glanced at the card, 'I'll manage thank you.'

With a brief goodbye, he left as abruptly as he had come. And once more the tiny office was empty and spacious. She could barely believe that he had actually gone — she half expected to see him come striding back with more instructions but all was quiet.

Feeling quite exhausted she allowed herself the luxury of putting her elbows on the desk and letting her head fall into her hands as she sighed. Would she be able to work with Richard Ellis? He was going to be very demanding. But if it didn't work out she need only see him during office hours. The rest of the time she would probably be in a nearby hotel where there would most likely be other business people to keep her company and her mind off her formidable boss.

Sitting there several minutes passed and then, realising that tomorrow was getting nearer by the second, she sprang up and started looking through her filing cabinets and desk. Gradually she gathered the papers and books she would need to take with her and when at last they were finally in her briefcase she gave a sigh of relief and walked into the shared hallway.

Armed with two cups of coffee from the machine she kicked at the identical office door next to her own. 'Okay to come in?' she called.

'Only if you are the bearer of coffee, strong and black.' The door opened and Mark's friendly grin was like the warmth of a fire after the cold manner of her last client. 'What the hell was going on in your office?'

'Just one very awkward man,' she explained. 'He's impatient, his manners are appalling but he has just one saving grace,' she grinned.

'Don't tell me, he's got a job for you!'

'That's right, but whether or not I can work for him, I just don't know.'

'Well love, that's something we all have to learn, to take the good clients with the bad.'

'He's very bad. As bad as you could

imagine,' she said despondently.

'Well then, cheer up because that means, with the law of averages, that your next one will be better than most.'

'If I wasn't desperate for money I wouldn't even think of working for him,' she said.

'Remember the personalities don't count. A client is just a client and a means to an end and the end is success.'

'I know that. It's not always easy to remember though.'

'It gets easier by the day. Believe me I know.'

She looked at Mark's calm smile and believed him although she couldn't help making comparisons between his dark almost classic good looks and the rugged fairness of the man who'd just left. Mark was one of her dearest friends but after Richard Ellis he seemed like a boy.

For half an hour they discussed what needed to be attended to while she was away. 'As soon as I can I'll send you my address. I expect when I arrive there tomorrow he will have booked me in somewhere.'

'How about dinner tonight before you go?'

She hesitated, wishing she could accept but knowing that there were a thousand and one things she'd have to do before tomorrow morning. 'Sorry I'd like that but there just isn't time.'

'Don't look so glum, it'll be much better than you think. You'll see.' Mark's glance was concerned and she read the affection in his eyes and wished she could return it.

The chores in her small apartment were soon done. It was the packing that took all her time. She knew that Richard's business was in the area of the New Forest in Hampshire and although her office clothes were standard, it was the leisure time that made her hesitate. Would she be able to indulge her love of walking at weekends? Would she need something smart for dinner at the hotel? Finally she packed a couple of cases with a selection of clothes to cover most eventualities.

At least her surroundings would be a bonus but as for the actual job anything could happen and probably would. Punching her pillow she rolled over, knowing that it was essential she had a good night's rest.

All she must do was remember he's the boss and ignore his temper and try not to be affected by his good looks. It was all going to be so simple.

2

Annie did not sleep well but lay uneasily with a nagging at the back of her senses that she couldn't quite place. Annie Ashley with the confidence to set up her own business was just plain scared.

At least the thought came to her as she quickly showered; it was going to be a beautiful day and she began to look forward to the journey. Dithering over what to wear she finally settled on jeans for driving and topped them with a toning blue shirt that brought out the depths of her eyes. Her reflection showed a girl of medium height with the tightness of her jeans accentuating well-shaped legs and rounded bottom. Deciding as usual to play down her appearance she used only the minimum of make-up with a touch of mascara and a hint of pale pink lipstick.

Seeing the shining thickness of hair

on her shoulders it was a temptation to leave it loose. For a few moments she tossed it this way and that, enjoying the way it swung against her cheeks. Finally, grabbing a large blue slide, she started to fasten the clip and suddenly everything fell into place. It was the thought of meeting Richard Ellis again that had worried her all night. Not just meeting him but working for him for several weeks. It wouldn't be easy if their meeting the day before was anything to go by.

Scrambling around, she whipped through breakfast and the last minute jobs. Then mentally checking everything that was necessary had been packed, put her suitcases and briefcase in the boot of her car. Then grabbing a bulky cream sweater and a map she was ready for the journey.

★ ★ ★

Driving leisurely she was surprised she'd never visited the New Forest before. Most of her childhood family holidays had been spent in the West Country of Devon and Cornwall. Then, once older, it had been the cheap package abroad with friends. Somehow the area she was now approaching had been completely missed.

On each side, the close-cropped floor of the forest was intermingled with gorse and ferns. While further away grass, trees and bushes stretched out to infinity in varying shades of green. The first sight of ponies caused her to stop and wind down her window. On the lush verge just ahead were two mares with their foals. Even to a city bred girl like herself she could tell that the long-legged babies were just weeks old.

Taking the turn for Brockenhurst and grinning like a child she drove across the ford, delighting in the faint swish of the water against her wheels. Suddenly all her doubts about the job disappeared. How could she fail to be anything but happy in such a lovely place?

Twice she made a wrong turn and then suddenly was at the entrance to a property which was well hidden behind a high hedge. Well this was it and hesitating for a moment, she hovered outside feeling ridiculously frightened. Trying to ignore the lurching of her stomach and gritting her teeth she turned the car into the gravelled access.

As she bumped her way over the cattle grid, her first glance at the building caused her to stop and check the address. Something must be wrong because here was a beautifully thatched, long, rambling house, certainly not something she'd imagined the overbearing and impatient man who was expecting her to have. *Olde Worlde charm just isn't in it*, she thought to herself, noting the latticed windows and well stocked flower beds. There must be two places with the same name, she thought, surely this couldn't be his address, or could it?

A glint of sunlight on metal caught her attention and tearing her eyes from the house she realised that something was directly in her path. She pulled up sharply behind a gleaming vehicle. There must be serious money here, was her first thought as she glanced first at the house and then the car that sat in the drive. Her eyes dropped to the front of her own ancient red car and instinctively she backed slightly away from the gleaming machine. There was no way she wanted to park anywhere near it. Talk about poor relations. Laughter bubbled up inside her. Maybe there was a tradesmen's entrance where she would feel more at ease.

Hearing a crunch of gravel Annie looked up, startled to see Richard Ellis approaching. Like herself he was wearing jeans and a blue shirt; in fact apart from the wide leather belt in his jeans they were practically dressed alike. The thought made her feel uncomfortable. He looked younger and casual and wondering how she appeared to him, wished now she'd driven down in a suit or at least something more formal.

'Are you actually going to get out of that car?' He opened the door and looked down at her.

'I hope I'm not late.' Ignoring his taunt she opted for politeness. He was still holding the door obviously waiting for her to join him on the gravelled drive. Flustered she gathered up her shoulder bag and tried to get out in as elegant a fashion as possible. Hoping she'd made a reasonably graceful exit. Annie slung her bag over her shoulder and straightened up. As her head jerked up, it was obvious he was quite literally eyeing her up and down. His glance travelled the length of her shapely legs and hesitated at the small waist before continuing up to her face.

'Quite an improvement,' he murmured, 'I wondered what was hidden under that awful jacket yesterday.'

Flushed and furious Annie searched desperately for a way to get her own back and knew there was only one thing to do or she would never be on equal terms with this man. Clenching her hands so tightly they hurt she forced herself to step right out of character and began her own appraisal. Starting at his trainers, her eyes ran up the long lean length of leg, then up to his chest, and on to the wide powerful shoulders. 'I agree,' she mimicked him neatly. 'Quite an improvement. You look more at home casually dressed than in a suit.'

His eyes narrowed. Showing he was annoyed. Feeling shocked at her own behaviour she wondered how long it would be before she was on her way back to London.

Then without warning the steely grey eyes became almost blue as he started to laugh. 'I didn't think you were capable of that,' he spluttered. 'I'd put you down as the prissy type!' he said cruelly and mockingly.

Feeling shocked at what had happened it was almost a relief to see he'd taken it so well. The situation was so completely ridiculous that she joined in the laughter and suddenly they were just two people sharing a joke. Two people who might even come to like each other.

'Okay, so you've made your point.' He held out his hand. 'We're on equal terms, Annie Ashley.'

Smiling back Annie let her hand lay in the warmth of his until she realised she was enjoying the feeling just a bit too much and snatched it away.

'Cases in the boot?'

'Well yes,' she hesitated.

'Come on then, have you got the keys?' It seemed the little truce was soon over and he was back to being his usual impatient self.

She went to offer him the keys and stopped. 'But where am I staying?'

'Here of course.' He looked at her as though she was a backward child.

'Here?' her voice croaked. 'But this is your home?'

'Brilliant deduction. Now I know why they recommended you for the job.'

'But I can't stay here. Not with you.

Why I . . . I . . . ' she stuttered.

'Frightened you'll be compromised?' He made no secret of his amusement. 'I was right. You are prissy after all.'

'Of course I'm not,' she snapped. 'It's just that I never expected . . . I mean I thought I'd be staying at a hotel.'

'Far better you stay here. It'll be easier to liaise about work and . . . ' he taunted. 'You don't have to worry about your reputation. My mother has agreed to move in for a few weeks.'

Damn the man. He'd succeeded in making her feel like a heroine from a Jane Austen novel who needed chaperoning. Why did she always manage to give him the wrong impression?

'That's fine then.' Jangling her keys she bent over to unlock her boot. Trying to give herself time to recover from the shock of knowing they would be under the same roof she took her time selecting the right key.

'Is this all?' He was very close and leaned over to grab a case in each hand. As he did so his arm brushed her shoulder making her uncomfortably aware of him.

Snatching her briefcase she scuttled after him trying to catch up his long stride. Then as though remembering someone was there he hesitated and moved to one side so they could walk together.

A small plump woman who was probably in her late fifties opened the door. As he introduced her to his mother there was very little resemblance between them. Certainly not in the warm smile and welcome the other woman gave her.

'You must be Annie, you don't mind if I call you that, do you? You must call me Laura. I'm so glad you've arrived as lunch is almost ready.'

Murmuring a reply she followed the woman into a square hall with a gleaming polished wooden floor.

'Show Annie to her room, Richard and get her settled in and then she can come down to the dining room.'

Smiling at his mother affectionately

he carried the two suitcases to a room at the back of the house delicately decorated in pink and white. The walls were washed the palest pastel pink, contrasting beautifully with the dark beams, which crossed the white ceiling. The furniture was simple, just a wardrobe, a matching desk and chair and a dressing table in pine. Matching curtains and duvet were flowered in two shades of rose while the soft carpet picked up the darker tone. The effect was feminine and pretty but at the same time very restful.

A slight rustle of the curtains drew her to the open window where she saw the garden backed on to open forest land. Annie leaned out, breathing deeply and the air smelled of grass and sun quite unlike the traffic-laden atmosphere of London.

'Do you like it? Through that door there is a small bathroom solely for your own use.'

Turning in surprise she realised she had quite forgotten the man. 'It's absolutely beautiful.'

'I'm so glad,' he said simply and Annie knew he meant it. 'Do you forgive me now for not booking you into a hotel?'

'Yes, of course. You have a lovely home.'

'I want you to be happy here, Annie.' He sounded absolutely sincere as though he was pleased she liked his house.

'Thank you. I'm sure I will be.'

'Richard,' he smiled. 'You must call me Richard.'

She was still smiling and puzzling at his change of attitude after he had left the room. Then leaving her unpacking until later she washed in the pink basin and deciding not to change, combed her hair, refastened the slide and made her way to the dining room.

★   ★   ★

She soon felt at ease in the company of Richard's mother who chatted through

31

lunch asking her about her home and family. Relaxing in the warmth of Laura's interest she spoke freely about her parents' early retirement to Cornwall where so many of her childhood holidays had been spent. And even found herself confessing that when her father sold his house on the outskirts of London he had given her a sum for a deposit on an apartment.

Glancing across at Richard she expected to find him bored with the lunchtime conversation and deep in his own thoughts. However the quietness from his side of the table showed rather that he was listening intently to what was being said and Annie had the odd feeling his mother was asking questions he'd like to ask her himself.

'So you're an only child as well as Richard.'

Suddenly Richard shoved back his chair. 'I'm going to go and get changed and head to the office.

'Sorry,' she sprang up. 'I'll go and change as well. You'll obviously want me to start work this afternoon.'

'No.'

'No?'

'No, not this afternoon. You'll need to unpack and get used to the place. Mother will show you round and tell you anything you need to know about the area.' For a moment it looked as though he was going to smile. 'You can come in with me tomorrow.'

She was obviously dismissed and sank back into her chair.

'You mustn't mind Richard,' Laura was talking quietly. 'I know how he must appear to you. But I assure you,' she smiled weakly, 'his bark is worse than his bite.'

'Well really but . . . '

Laura rose, 'Don't think too badly of him, he's had a very difficult time. I'll get some coffee and we'll take it outside.'

During the afternoon she learned a lot about Richard from his mother. Obviously proud of her only son, the older woman explained that his father's health started to break down just as Richard was about to go to university. He gave up his studies to keep the family business going. 'We had just the one boat chandler's then, Jack sank all his money into it after he left the merchant navy. It was a good living and enough for us.'

'But it's a large chain now,' Annie said gently.

'Oh yes. Richard took it over when my husband died. He'd recently married and built it up to what it is today. He seemed to work day and night. When he started the second shop I thought it would stop there but he went on adding to it with a single mindedness that at times quite worried me. But as you can see it paid off.'

Quite suddenly her mouth dried, so the man was married! But what was she thinking about, she was only here to work. The set up was just too cosy, he should have let her go to a hotel. Aware that Laura was looking at her, she forced her voice to respond. 'Does he still work so hard?'

'Yes but at least he has his boat. After Katie, it's the great interest in his life and at least that gets him away from the business. Everyone needs time to relax, even my son.'

For the second time she swallowed nervously, so he was married to someone called Katie, but where was this woman? She pushed her thoughts to one side and the afternoon passed pleasantly with a tour of the house and gardens. A swimming pool discreetly shielded by trees was not allowed to intrude upon the old fashioned charm. Then gloriously beyond that was the open forest. Briefly Annie wondered just how successful you had to be to own all this.

She was not surprised when they dined alone. In spite of telling herself that Richard's private life was of no interest to her she couldn't resist trying to picture the type of woman who would appeal to him.

Later she left Laura to the television

and settled herself in another room. Curling up in an oversized armchair she read through some notes to prepare herself for the morning but her thoughts wandered. Why wasn't his wife here and why had he needed his mother to come and stay?

Laying the papers aside she relaxed for a few moments marvelling at the utter quietness of the night. Then the silence was broken with the throaty roar of a car which throttled back as it turned into the drive and stopped with a crunch of gravel. Now wishing she'd gone to bed earlier she hoped Richard would go straight to his room and could avoid seeing him until tomorrow. That would be soon enough she thought wryly.

But just as she'd known it would, the door opened and the peace of the night was broken.

'Drink?' he asked her without bothering with a greeting.

'No, thank you.' It was said rather more primly than intended. 'I was just about to go to bed.'

'Oh, stay for a few minutes.'

Watching him pour himself a whisky Annie wished suddenly she'd accepted his offer of a drink. It would give her something to do instead of just sitting there.

'Tell me,' he asked. 'Do you like the water?' He settled himself in the chair opposite her.

'Water,' she repeated frowning.

'Yes,' he snapped impatiently. 'Swimming, boats all that sort of thing. It's the main social occupation here, unless you ride?'

'No, I don't ride.' It was said abstractedly with part of her mind thinking about his previous question. Water sports, they would account for his healthy outdoor complexion.

'Well as you live in town, I didn't expect you did. How about boats, there's plenty of gravel pit sailing near to London.'

'No, I don't know much about boats either. In fact, well . . . I'm ashamed to admit that I can't even swim.'

'You must come out in the boat. We'll take a trip across to France. You'll love it but I'll teach you to swim first.'

Annie gaped unable to believe this was happening

Once again wishing she'd accepted a drink, she said, 'I've come to do a job of work not take jaunts across the channel.'

'You need to let your hair down once in a while.'

He was looking at her hair so intently as though he were imagining it loose and flowing. For a minute she even thought he was going to get up and unfasten her slide. Knowing she should leave the room but quite unable even to leave the chair, she was motionless knowing that whatever he did she'd be unable to stop him.

Then he reached for his whisky glass and the spell was broken. Cursing her vulnerability she turned so that her expression was hidden.

'Ah,' he teased, 'you know what they

say about all work and no play.'

'I'm not here to play.' She began to shuffle the papers and her notes together and place them in a file.

'A little bit of relaxation is good for everyone. No one can work at the same pace forever. I tried that once myself,' he continued. 'I work hard but I make sure I play hard as well. You should learn how to play, Annie.'

Feeling strongly that the conversation was getting out of hand she stood up. 'There'll be plenty of time for play when I'm more established.'

'Don't leave it too long,' he said, taunting her. 'There may not be anyone left to play with.'

'This conversation is absurd,' she said indignantly. 'I assure you that my life, both business and social, is quite well balanced.'

She gave him a long level look as she said, 'Good night.' But when she closed the door he was laughing and she knew it would take more than a level look to stop him teasing her.

Resolving not to be alone with him more than could be helped Annie crawled under the duvet. It had been a day of contrasts with the unexpected charm of Richard's home and the warm friendliness of his mother.

She thought about her own hobbies of reading and walking and decided that if he did ask her out on his boat she would be too busy doing her own thing. He wasn't the type to keep asking if she kept refusing. He wouldn't waste his time on her.

But then she remembered he was supposed to be married. Was the outing to be a merry threesome? She didn't think so. But what about Katie? What about Richard's wife?

3

There was a clean freshness in the air when Annie awoke which made her think there had been rain at some point during the night.

Leaning out of her window it seemed there had indeed been a light shower in the night and now the garden and adjoining forest was freshly washed and new. Dressing quickly in jeans and a soft white sweater she crept downstairs.

Walking swiftly to the path she'd noticed yesterday, the one which led to the forest, Annie was amazed at the beauty of the area. *If only I could bottle this air and take it back,* she mused, breathing deeply. *I would make a fortune and not have to worry about computers.* Picking her way over the cattle grid she glanced around deciding to make this early morning walk a habit. The dampness of the grass shimmered in the clear light, thick and lushly green, washed by the slight fall of rain. Checking her watch she turned reluctantly and hurried back along the path to the house. Another movement caught her attention and pausing behind a screen of trees she saw Richard walking briskly towards the back door. A short black towelling robe covered most of his body but long, well-muscled brown legs caused her a moment's embarrassment and she watched him reach the house before she moved.

Gaining the safety of her room she started to prepare for the day ahead, and for a moment was tempted to put on a light, pretty dress. Managing to push the thought away she opened her wardrobe and took out a grey outfit. Later, inspecting her rather formal and businesslike appearance in the mirror, she knew it had been the right choice.

Entering the dining room she faltered and met amused grey eyes that quickly travelled over her suit and crisp shirt.

Giving him as bright a smile as she could manage Annie sat down relieved to see Laura bringing a tray of coffee and toast.

Refusing the offer of a cooked breakfast she chatted to Laura, noticing out of the corner of her eye that Richard was also dressed in an extremely formal way which made her feel more relaxed and confident. He said very little, appearing to be engrossed in the paper much to the dismay of his mother who chided him gently about being rude to their guest.

'Annie isn't exactly a guest, mother,' he said abruptly as he left. As he reached the door he tossed over his shoulder. 'Be in the drive at 8.30.'

Her colour rose and she thanked her lucky stars that she hadn't put on a dress after all. His unkind remark had certainly put her right back in her place of an employee. In future she would be very much on her guard where he was concerned.

Laura looked helplessly at her. 'Don't

take any notice of him my dear, he has a lot going on at the moment and although he would never admit it, I think that now and again things get on top of him.'

'It's all right, don't worry about me. I understand. A lot of my clients are like that,' which was quite untrue. Then she quickly changed the subject completely by telling the older woman about her early morning walk.

Exactly at 8.30 Annie was in the drive to see Richard putting things in the back of his car. Straightening up when he saw her, he looked at the keys in her hand. 'You don't need those. You'll be coming with me.'

Being alone with him in that monster of a car was not something she relished. 'But I thought we'd go separately,' she tried to think of reasons to avoid being driven by him. 'That way you don't have to bring me home if you want to stay late, or go out, or anything,' her voice finished weakly.

'I've thought of all that,' he swiftly

dealt with her argument, pushing it aside as being unimportant. Opening the passenger door his foot tapped impatiently as he waited for her to get in.

This was not the time to argue and aware of his watching eyes Annie sank into luxury. Fighting the desire to admire the interior she immediately strapped herself in and in her haste fumbled slightly with the unfamiliar safety belt hoping that he didn't offer to help. Still smarting from his earlier thoughtless remark she expelled a sigh of relief when he walked round to his own side.

Then from the corner of her eye, she noticed another car draw up and a girl about 10 or 11 tumble out. A tall child with long fair hair.

'Hi Dad,' the figure rushed to Richard who swung her up off the ground.

'You're late Katie.'

'I know, but it was a brilliant sleep-over and Lucy's mother is going to run me to school when I've collected some stuff I need.' Then the girl saw Annie who was watching through the open window.

'I'll introduce you to Annie this evening, so get moving and say good morning to Granny.' He gave the child a shove and she ran into the house.

Annie sat motionless, so this was Katie and she was his daughter but where was the child's mother?

Eventually they got away and he drove slowly through the quiet roads but the power was there. It waited to be unleashed, held carefully in check as he meticulously observed the road signs. Power in check, she mused, and that was exactly how she would describe the owner.

Having already decided that he would be a fast and impatient driver, it was a surprise to find how aware and considerate he was of the animals at the side of the roads. Hmm . . . she fought back a giggle, fond of his mother and animals, that's something in his favour.

Misinterpreting the small sound he glanced quickly at her. 'Nervous?' he asked casually, once again making her feel school girlish. The wretched man sounded like an uncle driving a reluctant child to school.

'Why should I be?' Her voice was even.

'New jobs have that effect on some people.'

'Not on me. I'm very used to new assignments.'

'Of course.' As he turned she caught the full force of his smile and all thought of a reply left her.

She fought against that smile and concentrated on the scenery, all too aware of the tension mounting between them. Watching him from under her lashes she noticed tiny little things like the length of his fingers on the steering wheel, how his hands looked tanned and masculine but at the same time well kept. As he drove, he looked about him as though checking on every tree and blade of grass. She began to wonder who was the real Richard; the business tycoon, the sportsman with his love of water or the country gentleman. He had a knack of switching roles at the drop of a hat.

There was no mention of the child and she didn't like to broach the subject in case she appeared to be too interested in his affairs. Any other man would surely have spoken about his daughter. The object of her thoughts began to speak. 'Spring is beautiful with the new born foals and,' he pointed through the windscreen, 'those large clumps of bright yellow gorse you can see everywhere.'

'Yes, I noticed them on the way down yesterday and again this morning when I went out early.'

'Ah, I thought I saw someone in the garden.' He chuckled. 'Tell me, were you hiding from me?'

Ignoring his taunt she asked, 'And in summer, what is it like in summer?'

'Beautiful, with tall wild foxgloves and all the shrubs and trees are so rich and full.' He turned to her. 'You could still be here at summer and then you'll understand what I mean. Now autumn,' he continued, 'that's one of my favourite times, when the leaves change colour just before they fall.' He stopped speaking and then suddenly continued thoughtfully, 'Perhaps you'll see autumn as well.'

Her heart was doing the strangest things and she desperately wanted to be here not only in summer but also in autumn when the leaves fell.

The following silence was strangely companionable and she settled back in her seat puzzling over this other side of her employer's character.

Her first impression of Richard's office was one of surprise at the few people he employed.

He hustled her along the main office, not bothering to introduce her to anyone. 'You'll get to know them all in time,' he muttered as they reached a lobby with two facing doors.

He dropped her arm and pointed to

the first door. 'This is for your use for as long as you are here.' His arm swung round. 'And this is mine.'

Her office was large and airy with two desks, one for general use and the other for her computer. Here was everything to make her job as easy as possible and she wondered who she had to thank for planning it so well.

Turning to ask him, the words were never spoken as she listened to a list of instructions ending with, 'I'm next door, try not to bother me more than you can help.'

He was back to his old abrupt manner and all the lovely sense of companionship had evaporated. It was as though he was telling her that this was his kingdom and he was very much the boss.

'Most of what you want is here in the files, anything else, just ask outside in the general office. As you can guess, I'm pretty busy.' Not waiting for a reply he swung round and strode to the door leaving her fuming in the middle of the room.

Probably I'll have to make an appointment to even see him. Who does he think he is anyway, treating me like an office junior? 'Try not to bother him indeed', the arrogance of the man, he'll learn that I can be just as self sufficient as him. Talk about being thrown in at the deep end and she flung her briefcase on the desk. Serve him right if I walked straight out. Perhaps that would teach him a lesson in manners. At last, fighting down her temper, she looked round the room again.

Her temper forgotten she hung up her jacket and unlocked her briefcase.

The morning was interrupted when Richard brought in a tall, dark haired man in his early thirties. As she looked up at the warm, kindly face she knew that she had found a friend. This was Steve, the accountant, who casually pulled up a chair to her desk and offered to take her through the system. Gratefully she agreed and as she listened she noticed that Richard had already disappeared. She knew that here was someone she could really get on with. He was open and friendly and as far as work went they spoke the same language.

During a working lunch of sandwiches and coffee they swapped information about themselves. He was not only Richard's accountant but also a friend and shared the same interest in boats. She watched him as he spoke, noting that although far less handsome he was very much easier to be with and thankfully he treated her as an equal.

After he left, Annie was much happier about everything and the afternoon flew by as she immersed herself in work. Absently she noted the 'goodbyes' from the office staff and, looking at her watch, realised that it was 7.00 p.m.

She stretched her back, flexing her stiff shoulders and wondered what time Richard usually went home. The place had an empty air about it and it crossed her mind that he could have already left but of course he wouldn't do that after bringing her in his car. Then, as though her thoughts had summoned him, the door opened and he crossed to her desk. Just as she was about to enquire as to what time they were leaving she looked up to see the puzzled expression in his eyes.

Quickly she relaxed her shoulders muttering, 'I'm a bit stiff.' What a silly comment to make and mentally kicked herself feeling flustered. Then her colour rose even more as, without moving his eyes, he walked around her chair to stand behind her.

'Allow me.' His hands were warm and firm across the back of her neck.

She jumped in surprise and immediately tensed her whole upper body.

'Relax.' His voice was low. 'I'm quite good at this. After a day on the boat we all get a bit stressed and this is a good way to get rid of the knots.'

His hands began a symphony, playing across her back, her neck and round to her upper arms. Kneading and stroking and draining out the tension and replacing it with a most delicious sensual feeling that was spreading through her whole body. Swallowing hard she fought the powerful urge to lean against him.

Just as she was beginning to sway backwards her mind cleared and she sat bolt upright shrugging him away. 'I'm fine now, thank you,' and wondered why he was still standing behind her and then as something brushed her neck she knew what he was about to do. Not knowing if she was unable to move or part of her didn't really want to move she felt him unfasten the slide that held her hair. He was running his fingers through the long strands and spreading them across her shoulders.

'I've wanted to do this since I first saw you, to see your hair loose.' He was so dangerously near that she could feel his warm breath on her cheeks.

This was no way to behave with a new employer but she was unable change her position. Why was she allowing such intimacies because business and pleasure she'd told herself time and time again, never mixed. But the thrilling awareness of his touch was impossible to fight and she was powerless to move away.

Turning her head she saw him hesitate and then draw back. 'No, not yet,' he muttered, more to himself than to her as he moved again.

Cursing her vulnerability and turning so that her expression was hidden, she hoped desperately that he didn't think she would be an easy conquest and gathering up her pride as best she could started to put papers away in her desk. 'Let's just stick to the job. That's what I'm here for. That's why you are paying me,' she shot at him in an effort to recover her poise.

'One day Annie,' he said quietly and it sounded like a threat.

In a daze she followed him out to the car and clutched her precious briefcase like a lifeline.

Cruising back through the forest he

broke the silence. 'Tell me what have you got against men?'

'Nothing,' she stammered.

'Then why the tied back hair, these awful suits?' He briefly touched her thigh where the grey skirt rested and she jumped as though he'd burned her. 'That's exactly what I mean. You jump like a frightened rabbit every time I'm near you. You play down your appearance as though you're trying to hide. What is it with you Annie?'

Furiously she turned on him. 'I'm a person in my own right, with a good brain and the ability to do a good job.'

He looked taken aback at her anger. 'Okay, so I teased you a bit when we first met. It's the natural reaction of a man to a pretty girl.'

'I don't want this,' she turned to him almost pleading. 'My life is set on a course and I don't want anything or anybody upsetting it. Can't you understand and leave me alone?'

'I'm sorry, Annie. Believe me when I say I didn't mean to upset you.'

'Let's just keep the relationship business-like, shall we?'

'I promise I'll keep it like that for just as long as you want me to.'

She turned to him suspiciously. 'What do you mean?'

'Just what I say.' He sounded ridiculously innocent. 'Of course,' he continued, 'any time you want to change that you'll only have to ask.'

Almost casually he said, 'Has some-one hurt you? Someone in the past?'

She hesitated. 'No, not me but a friend.'

'Care to tell me about it?'

'No.' It was said abruptly

'Just no.'

'Definitely no.'

The rest of the journey was spent in silence although she knew that he looked across at her from time to time. Once, glancing at him, she was surprised at the concern on his face and then fearing that he was going to speak she quickly feigned interest in some-thing she saw through her window.

At last the car stopped and she mentally calculated the time before she could decently retire to her room.

'There's one thing you can't hide.' His voice had that infuriating teasing quality. 'You may tie back your hair, wear awful clothes, but you can't hide those beautiful blue eyes.'

'Stop it, damn you!' she exploded with her hand on the door. Then once again remembered he was married. He acted so much like a single man that it was hard to remember he had a wife. 'You disgust me!' her voice rose, 'You're supposed to be married with a child so keep away from me. I'm not interested in married men.' Without even bothering to shut her door, she rushed from the car, charged into the house and nearly ran right into Katie; the child looked at her suspiciously.

'This is Annie,' Richard had come in behind her. 'Who's staying here for a time while she does some work for me.'

'Hello Katie,' she extended a hand and the child took it in an adult fashion but after a brief 'Hi,' turned away. *Oh dear*, thought Annie, *I haven't made much of a hit there, the girl is as difficult as her father and with the same steel-grey eyes.*

That night she excused herself early and took work to her room. Expecting to be in a hotel she'd also brought a couple of paper backs and determined to spend as much time alone as possible. Dinner had been an ordeal while she struggled to eat the lovely meal that Laura had prepared, not wanting to worry the older woman by letting her see how upset she was. Richard, she noticed angrily, was his usual casual self and chatted mainly to his daughter who was full of the sleep-over with her friends the previous night. It was as though nothing got through that tough hide of his, not where she was concerned anyway.

4

The pressure was off next morning at breakfast; Laura told Annie,

'Richard sends his apologies he's been called away.'

Sitting down abruptly she understood the full meaning of the word reprieve as a wave of well being flowed gently over her.

'Such a pity,' Laura continued, 'You'll have to drive yourself. Are you sure you can find the way?'

Suddenly the world was wonderful, the coffee smelled delicious, the toast was golden and she was starving hungry. Could she drive herself? Oh yes, most definitely and with the greatest of pleasure.

'It's forecast for a very hot day. Do use the pool if you wish.'

'I'm afraid I don't swim,' she admitted ruefully biting into yet another piece of toast. 'I don't even possess a swim suit.'

'Why don't you practise while you're here? I'm sure you'd find it very relaxing after a day at the office.' Laura topped up their cups with coffee.

Why not, the thought entered her head knowing there wouldn't be anyone to mock her feeble attempts. 'Does Katie's mother swim?' There, she'd asked the question and hoped it sounded casual, then without waiting for a reply, rushed on. 'It's a lovely idea, thank you Laura, but is there anywhere I could buy a swim suit?'

'I'm going into Southampton today, if you told me your size and what you wanted I could get something for you.' Laura hesitated. 'I wondered if Richard had mentioned his family to you but as you're staying here, you ought to know. We don't talk about his wife; she went off with another man when Katie was a baby. Of course they're divorced and during the week Katie lives with me. I have a place nearby. It's not ideal,' she seemed to want to go on. 'I hope one day Richard will marry again but, I think it will be Katie's choice. He adores her and would never have her upset.'

'Oh, I'm so sorry.' Annie now found she felt distinctly uncomfortable.

'Don't worry my dear, we're all used to the situation now. Anyway back to your swimsuit what would you like?'

After confirming her size and deciding on something dark and plain she left the breakfast table feeling much happier than when she first came in.

His mother was an absolute pet and he obviously didn't take after her so perhaps his father had been a difficult man. She'd never know and it didn't matter to her. This was only a short episode in her life and she should make the best of it. Besides she was young and it was a lovely day and there was an interesting job in front of her. What more could a girl want from life?

Humming as she drove, Annie found her way to the office without any trouble and parked neatly in the space reserved and marked RE. After all he wouldn't be in and there was something very satisfying about leaving her own car in the spot where his shining one usually stood.

* * *

She was just wondering whether to send out for some sandwiches again for lunch when Steve arrived and solved the problem in the nicest way.

'Can you take a break yet?' His friendly face smiled at her. 'I know Richard is away and thought you might like to come to lunch with me.'

Suddenly an hour away from her desk seemed very attractive especially in the easy undemanding company of the accountant. 'What a lovely idea, I can break any time you like.'

'Good, come on then, I know a great pub but it's advisable to be there early as it gets very crowded.'

As he settled her in his Volvo Estate

she glanced across at her own car, standing defiantly in its privileged parking space.

Steve caught her eye and grinned. 'I see you like living dangerously.'

'Absolutely, it gives life a bit of spice.' She crossed her fingers and they were both chuckling companionably as they turned on to the road.

Later, sitting at the tiny round table waiting for Steve to bring their food from the bar she was even more glad to be there. The place was picturesque with the bar having attractive low beams with brasses decorating almost every part of the walls. While just behind her the large open fireplace had a cool spectacular arrangement of leaves and flowers in a large copper bowl.

'What wicked calories,' she looked at his large plate of chips and sausages and then smugly at her own salad.

'I get the message,' he laughed. 'I'm afraid food is one of my weaknesses. But I don't smoke and I drink very little, which only leaves food — or women, of course.'

'Have you got plenty of women in your life?' Annie teased, wondering how it was possible to feel so at ease with him. She studied him across the table. He was really quite attractive in his own way and very good company. What's more he was obviously enjoying being with her which was very good for her morale.

'Yes,' he answered, 'all dark and sultry, but,' he looked at her silky fair hair, 'I think I could be persuaded to change to blondes.'

A change of subject was obviously needed and on an impulse she leaned across the table and said, 'I'm finding Richard quite difficult to work with.'

'What, Richard?' He looked amazed. 'He's got a brilliant brain and masses of drive. Most people find him stimulating and I'm very happy to be his accountant. I find we're on the same wavelength, although,' he hesitated, 'I have to keep him in check as his enthusiasm sometimes outruns his good sense.'

Annie watched as Steve continued in full flood and thought what a staunch and loyal friend he was. 'But women,' she asked when she could get a word in edgewise. 'What of other women, do they find him difficult?'

'Oh women,' he shrugged and paused to take another mouthful of food. 'They're always attracted to him, not just by his looks but by his success. You're the first one who's ever said he's difficult. I say, this is awfully good.' He looked at her plate of salad. 'How's your food?'

'Quite adequate,' she laughed. 'If that's what you're hinting.'

There was silence for a while as they ate and then a disturbance at a nearby table caused them both to look in that direction. Two men and a girl had just entered the bar.

'Talking about women,' murmured Steve. 'That is one lady who is very interested in your boss.'

Annie followed his gaze to see a smallish, voluptuous woman seating herself at the table. Medium length dark hair surrounded a pale triangular face with a full wide mouth. 'Who is she?' she whispered.

'That's Pascale Saunders, daughter of Saunders the boat builders.' He pushed his plate away. 'That was good. Fancy a dessert?'

She shook her head. 'I never eat it.'

'They do some wonderful chocolate concoctions,' he persuaded.

Losing the battle with her conscience she nodded. 'But not too rich.' If she swam in the pool tonight and started her morning walks again she would soon work off the extra calories.

Annie studied the dark woman from under her lashes. The lady was stunning all right, it wasn't only her looks but an air of total confidence that drew everyone's eyes. Whilst talking, she shrugged her shoulders and used her hands in charmingly expressive gestures. 'That dark woman,' she asked as

Steve returned, 'is she foreign?'

'Half and half,' he delved into his dessert with gusto. 'Father's English but the mother is French.'

She remembered Richard asking if she spoke French and then saying in that casual way he was fluent. Was this woman the reason? Annie continued to watch, fascinated with the continual movements of the fluttering hands. She hardly realised she was staring until, as though she knew she was being watched, the woman turned glittering coal-like eyes upon her. Hurriedly Annie looked away but out of the corner of her eye could see that the dark woman was getting up and coming in their direction.

'Pascale is coming over,' Steve said matter of factly. 'I'll introduce you.' His tone lowered, 'Then you can see what type appeals to Richard.'

'No, don't get up Steve.' The words were low and sultry. 'I don't think I know your friend.' The coal eyes turned to Annie again.

'This is Annie Ashley. Annie, meet Pascale Saunders.'

The two women murmured polite greetings and sized each other up.

'When is Richard coming back?' Pascale turned to Steve as though dismissing Annie as of no significance.

'Not sure, but I don't think he'll be away long as Annie has just started.'

Pascale swung round. 'Oh, you're the one working for Richard.' Her voice had sharpened.

'I'm a Computer Consultant.' Annie lifted her chin not liking the attitude of the other girl. 'I'm helping Richard update his system.'

'Oh, those computers, I've never really understood them.' She shrugged making Annie feel that to work with computers was the most unfeminine job anyone could choose. 'But I know he's worried about the work. I have a boutique near to Richard's office. You must come and look at my clothes sometime.' The gaze that travelled over Annie's neat office suit was taunting and superior.

'If I have the time.' She matched the attitude of the dark eyed woman and turned to continue her desert leaving Steve to do all the talking.

'Katie loves clothes you know and she loves to come to my boutique. Of course we're very close.' Pascale just fired off the sentence at Annie before turning back to Steve. Eventually giving a brief nod goodbye she watched the girl make her way back to her own table. She had that chic something that was the envy of every woman and in contrast she made Annie feel frumpy and ordinary.

'Stunning isn't she?' Steve was watching Pascale's swaying hips in her tight blue dress.

'Very, and that's the type he likes, is it?'

'That's very much the type he likes.'

Although she joined in the laughter, Annie felt a bit hollow as she looked across at the other table. Her own fair looks wouldn't stand a chance against the sultry darkness of Pascale. But why should that worry her? It wasn't as though she was interested, was it?

After all, Richard was nothing to her. She didn't like him and certainly didn't fancy him. In fact, he was everything she disliked in a man. Nevertheless the thought of him and Pascale was somehow disturbing.

Arriving back at the office something nagged at the back of her mind. Pascale had said that Richard was worried about the work. Surely she didn't mean that he was worried about her ability to do the job. If something went wrong on a job Gallings passed to her, then her business would be in a critical state. Pushing the idea away, she decided to put it out of her mind.

But there was still a slight unease which she couldn't dispel and had difficulty concentrating on the job. Gathering up her papers she remembered her conversation with Laura. If she'd managed to get a swimsuit, she could relax in the pool before dinner.

Laura had indeed bought a swimsuit but it wasn't quite what Annie intended. Looking at the minuscule black bikini she swallowed and wondered how much of her it would actually cover.

'Is it all right dear?' Laura questioned anxiously. 'The sales girl assured me this is what young people are buying. And of course when I told her how fair you were she suggested the black.'

'It's very nice,' she managed. The young people could well be teenagers who were not quite so generously curved as herself. The thing to do now was to try and make some excuse not to swim but lifting the hair from her neck with a warm hand, the thought of the pool was certainly enticing. Looking at Laura she thought, *what the hell, no one is here but us two women so it didn't matter one bit whether it covered well or not*. 'I'll run and put it on and if you promise not to watch my pathetic attempts I'll try it out. A splash around in the pool is just what I can do with at the moment.'

Could the sexy blonde with the loosened hair and two minuscule pieces of black bikini really be her? Annie posed in front of the mirror. 'Pascale eat your heart out,' she muttered under her breath giggling then, grabbing a large towel from the bathroom, ran quickly down the stairs.

Wishing she could dive or at least have the courage to jump into the water she gingerly edged down the steps. For a few moments she hung on to the bar but as her confidence grew she stepped backwards and tried a few tentative strokes.

She repeatedly backed further away from the edge and tried to swim to the bar. She was up to four strokes when she lost her breath and, splashing and spluttering, made a grab for the rail. Shaking the water from her face she glanced up to see a pair of large brown feet standing just above her.

'So you've taken my advice.'

'About what?' Annie tried to duck under the water and hide the revealing bikini from his eyes.

'About swimming of course.'

Instead of answering, she stretched out for her towel. Just as her fingers reached it a brown foot kicked it completely out of her reach.

'Why you . . . ' Her voice rose with the effort of trying to lever herself out.

'Oh, no you don't, I've come to give you a lesson,' he told her.

Annie gulped. A swimming lesson with him was something she could well do without. Just the thought of his hands anywhere near her briefly clad body would doubtless cause her to drown, at the very least.

'I've had enough now,' she tried to speak casually. 'So if you'd just pass my towel I'll come out.' Then something appeared to arch over her and dive into the deeper part of the pool. Really this was too much, the only reason she'd ventured out here was because he was supposed to be away.

'Laura said you were away,' she snapped as he surfaced beside her.

'Yes but I had to go to the Isle of Wight first and I was so long there I decided to come home tonight and go off again first thing in the morning.' As he was speaking he cupped her chin in his hand.

'Keep away from me,' she shoved at his large immovable body.

'Do you think that you are so irresistible that every man who gets within a foot of you has to be pushed away?' His other arm was at the front of her waist. 'Contrary to your supposition, I'm only giving you a swimming lesson. Just let yourself float forward and I'll support you.'

It was said so casually that she found she was obeying his instructions and laying on the water supported by him at her stomach and chin. Richard's voice was telling her how to breathe and use her arms and legs. There was nothing sexual in his touch and she began to relax and enjoy herself. When eventually there was just the support of his hand at her chin she felt she was really accomplishing something.

'Not bad for a beginner,' he quipped.

'I think I'm doing pretty well,' she panted reaching the side. His grin was the last straw and unthinkingly she splashed him, taking great satisfaction in seeing him swallow a mouthful of water.

'You won't get away with that.' He returned the splash with force.

She made for the steps but he caught her and ducked her under and she came up with water streaming from her mouth and eyes. As he started to swim away she grabbed his foot and tugged it but he somersaulted out of reach to return again scooping up handfuls of water and splashing her face and hair. Soon the whole area echoed with their laughter as they played like children. Her hair was hanging around her shoulders like damp seaweed and she could smell that strange bleach-type smell peculiar to most pools. Richard's eyes were bright and clear and full of glee and she wondered why she'd ever felt afraid of this man who was behaving like an overgrown schoolboy. It must be years since she'd played like this with the simple fun of childhood. At last Richard levered himself out and reached down to pull her up with him.

It was then that the electricity charged between them. Standing before him he raked her with his eyes from head to toe. 'So this is what is hidden under those awful suits.' His face flushed slightly across his cheekbones. 'I must say this is a definite improvement. I imagined you in a schoolgirl one piece, sort of jolly hockey, if you know what I mean. It just goes to show how women are all surprises.'

'Why you . . . '

Grey eyes challenged blue and at the same time they both became aware of a subtle change, a softening of glance, a swift, sensual awareness that sent the colour flooding to her face. He didn't touch her, he didn't need to; slowly her will was breaking and she was spinning out of control. Now she couldn't remember why she hated him but was only aware of eyes that now locked with hers, eyes asking questions and demanding answers.

'Hi you two! Granny said fifteen minutes to dinner.' It was Katie and she was looking at them in a very knowing way. 'Why aren't you in the pool?'

'Is this what they mean by being saved by the bell?' he murmured quietly in her ear. 'Or should we say the dinner gong.' Then he turned to his daughter, 'I thought you would be joining us. Never mind, perhaps tomorrow we can all swim together.'

It completely changed the mood and she felt her shoulders sag and her mouth turn up as laughter bubbled inside her. Then his deeper voice joined in and they were laughing together as though they would never stop.

'What's so funny?' Katie asked suspiciously.

'Oh, It's just that Annie can't swim very well.'

'I'm not really surprised,' said Katie

78

in a grown up manner and turned back to the house.

Annie gasped in annoyance. 'Thanks for the vote of confidence.'

He laughed and picking up the white towel, wrapped it carefully round her and together they left the pool.

The meal was delicious and swimming had given her an appetite. Dinner was a relaxed and friendly affair quite different from the undertones of the previous night. There was just one strained moment when she told Richard about lunching with Steve and meeting Pascale in the bar. He frowned as though he disapproved but whether it was from her meeting with Steve or Pascale being there she didn't know.

'Pascale is cool,' Katie piped up, 'and her shop is wild.'

All in all, she mused, as she prepared for bed, it was one of the nicest meals she'd had in a long while. A real friendly, family meal with plenty of teasing and banter, which made her realise how much she was missing her own family. Perhaps she'd judged Richard too harshly. Today he'd played and teased and been fun.

Her last thoughts were what a lovely mother-in-law Laura would make some lucky girl. Perhaps it would be Pascale but it was really nothing to do with her. After all Katie obviously admired Pascale and for some reason seemed to resent Annie and certainly didn't want to be friends with her.

5

The next morning she woke early and was strangely anxious to see Richard before he left. Dressing swiftly she raced to the top of the stairs. Then pride made her slow down and deliberately place each foot slowly and carefully on the treads.

Peering through the tiny panes in the hall, she could see his car but suddenly there was the noise of the engine and she knew she'd missed him and he was leaving.

Without him, the week rolled quietly into the weekend and out into a new week. Katie was occupied with friends and almost ignored her when she was at home. She'd had a vague idea that she and the child should do something together but obviously she was not cool enough for Katie.

So when Monday came again she was

restless and eager to be at work and feeling fed up she again parked in Richard's reserved space, telling herself it was a perk of the job. Steve lightened her day by asking her out the following evening. 'A lovely thatched restaurant with superb food,' he coaxed as though he could sense her hesitation.

Annie was tempted to refuse to go out with Steve, as it would be nice to be there when Richard came home. Then common sense asserted itself, how would she feel if he found out she had refused an invitation. Would he guess it was because she wanted to be with him? But why should he?

Eventually she agreed to go with Steve because there was no real reason to refuse but she didn't feel particularly wholehearted about it.

★　★　★

Richard returned the following afternoon. He was obviously in a bad mood and everything she'd built up about him in her mind came tumbling down. Only one thought got her through the day; she was glad to be going out that evening.

For from the moment she saw him, he was completely impossible.

Feminine intuition sent her eyes snapping up to see him framed in the office doorway. Immediately something warm and lovely ran through her entire body as she thought how much fairer he looked in his dark business suit with a grey and blue striped shirt adding depth to his eyes. In fact there was a certain brooding expression in those eyes she didn't understand. Then it was as though a shutter came down and without any greeting he strode up to her desk. 'What's your car doing in my parking space?'

She searched her mind for a reason. The bit of light hearted fun in leaving her car in his space now seemed childish. 'I'm sorry, I wasn't thinking.'

'I'd appreciate it if you remembered in future. I do like to drive straight into my own space.' He hesitated, and then added more kindly, 'There's room for your car surely.'

'Yes, of course.' She smiled and quickly changed the subject, 'Did you have a good trip?'

'So, so,' he muttered turning away. 'Any problems?'

'Yes a few, perhaps you could . . . '

'Later.'

He was gone, leaving her utterly deflated. Here was a master of the art of putting people down. One abrupt word brushed them aside as if they were of no importance. In her case this was obviously true. For a moment her shoulders sagged and her energy drained away. Like a fool she'd looked forward to him coming home, thinking they would pick up where they left off, but all that friendliness had disappeared and he was back to his old self.

The printer was churning out a programme and the noise masked the opening of the door but she knew when he entered the room once more. A stubborn streak forbade her to look up and greet him. He must make the first move. She'd had enough of his rude and abrupt manner earlier. Holding on tightly to her concentration she channelled her mind to think only of the figures being imputed into the machine. Damn the man, let him speak first, she was his equal and refused to be put in a subordinate position.

Why didn't he say something? Why was he just standing there? In a moment she would have to look up and acknowledge his presence. This couldn't be kept up much longer as already her neck ached from the tension she was creating for herself.

Just as her nerves were stretched to capacity, the telephone on her other desk rang and Richard moved to answer it. The moment was saved and she relaxed her shoulders as she listened to him speak.

'Yes, she's here,' he barked, obviously his temper had not improved during the afternoon. 'It's for you,' he turned to her holding the receiver.

Springing up she grabbed the telephone and, deliberately turning her back on him, leaned against the desk as casually as she could manage.

It was Mark, who chatted at length asking her how the job was going and if she had received the last lot of messages he'd sent to her by post. With only half her mind on Mark's voice she nearly missed the point of the call and then reaching for a pad she flipped it open.

'Go ahead, I'm ready.' She quickly wrote a name and address and a few details while cradling the phone under her chin.

'Thanks Mark, that's great.' Replacing the receiver and swinging round with shining eyes she forgot her anger. 'An enquiry for another job has come in.' She spoke quickly expecting Richard to share in her excitement.

'When for?' He snapped. 'You haven't finished working for me yet.'

'It's just an enquiry but could lead to

something big. In any case,' she added, 'it's going well here and I won't have to stay much longer.'

'I might want some extra work done.'

'Well, I could come back,' she frowned at his petulant tone.

'I don't want you thinking about other jobs in my time. I've got a business to run.'

'Of all the selfish, egotistical men, you are the worst I've ever met,' she exploded advancing towards him in her temper. 'I might remind you that I've got a business to run as well. A business that needs continuity of work just the same as any other.'

'I'm paying for your time.' He was almost shouting and she flinched as though the words were a physical attack.

But she wasn't going to back down. 'And you are damn well getting your money's worth.' She had to stop using that kind of language or she'd be swearing her head off soon.

Surprised at her outburst he lowered his voice. 'I won't be if you're making other arrangements while you're here. In any case, nothing has been proved yet, there maybe some snags to iron out.'

Again there was that slight inference that all might not be well with her work, once from Pascale and now from Richard himself. Her heart sank, for a good report from here could be necessary for her survival.

But again she flung them from her mind and faced him. 'There are some problems we need to discuss.' She crossed to a filing cabinet, extracted some papers and spread them over her desk. 'If you'd just like to look at these. I've underlined where the problem areas occur.'

However once his attention was caught he was all businessman and then arguments were forgotten as their discussion grew. In fact by the time they left the office they were on fairly friendly terms.

★ ★ ★

That evening he must have been delayed because she arrived at the house before him and after a quick coffee with Laura rushed up to shower and change. It would be nice to have a relaxing evening with Steve. They were easy and comfortable together. He was pleasant and undemanding and she took extra pains with her appearance wanting to please him.

After blow-drying her hair in loose, shining waves she applied her eye shadow and two coats of mascara and stood back pleased with the result. Her eyes looked huge and sultry and not wanting to detract from them she drew just a very pale lipstick across her mouth. Grinning, she wondered if Steve would recognise her from the rather primly dressed companion he took to lunch. Desperately hoping for some unknown reason to get away and out of the house before Richard saw her, she ran quietly down to the hall.

Laura had obviously been waiting and came from the kitchen smiling.

'How nice you look my dear.'

She turned with pleasure, grateful for the other woman's comment.

'Very nice,' a voice drawled from the study doorway. 'I hear you're going out with Steve. Is all this just for him?' His eyes roamed over her, taking in the elegant dress in muted shades of dark rose. The long-sleeved, low-necked bodice hugged her body while the full skirt flowed gracefully against her slim calves. Slender heeled shoes completed the outfit. 'The man will wonder what's hit him. The office duckling has turned into a veritable swan.'

Ignoring him she quickly checked her bag for make up and keys, desperately needing to be out of the house and out of reach of his taunting words. This was a terrible performance, especially in front of Laura.

'Did you know, Mother that Annie collects accountants — not content with one at home, she has to acquire one here as well.'

'Richard, really.' This appeared to be

Laura's stock phrase whenever she disapproved of her son's behaviour but this time her voice was low and there was amusement in her eyes. 'I think it's very nice for Annie to be taken on an evening out.'

'It's all right mother, it's just a joke.' He picked up Annie's wrap which was lying ready on the hall table. 'Allow me,' he came close behind her and she tensed knowing he would deliberately touch her. She could almost feel his warm breath as he bent his head, causing the back of her neck to prickle. Yes she was right and as the soft woollen fabric was placed on her shoulders his thumbs feathered against each side of her neck. Trembling at the lightness of his touch she once more fought a desire to lean back against him and feel his arms around her. He smoothed the wrap over her shoulders and down her arms. It was all very innocent to any one watching but she knew it was as far from innocence as he could get.

The sound of crunching gravel lifted the atmosphere and brought her quickly to her senses. Shrugging off his touch she ran to the door and grasped the handle as though it were a lifeline.

'Isn't Steve coming in for a drink?' Laura asked looking faintly puzzled.

'We're late,' she answered quickly, not knowing what time their table was booked, but some sixth sense warned her not to let the two men meet.

Steve appeared slightly startled as she rushed from the house. 'Is everything all right, you look a bit flustered?'

'Everything's fine. I didn't want to be late, that's all.'

From time to time he glanced at her as they drove but it wasn't until they arrived at the restaurant that the full impact of her appearance hit him. 'Annie,' he began and then appeared to dry up.

As she raised questioning eyebrows he continued. 'You look beautiful, I never realised . . . sorry, that didn't come out right . . . I mean to say . . . '

It was such an odd compliment that she laughed, explaining that she liked to play down her appearance in the office, as it was more businesslike. As they were shown to their table Annie was able to switch the conversation to safer channels. For a while they discussed work, two logical and mathematical minds that were on the same wavelength.

'I must be the world's biggest fool.' Steve looked at her ruefully. 'Here I am with a lovely girl and what do I talk about, business.'

From across the table she laid her hand briefly on his, 'I enjoyed it, I really did. It helped to put some of my thoughts in order.'

'But no more for the rest of the evening. The subject is closed. Agreed?'

'Agreed.' She laughed in reply.

Later, after an excellent meal and two glasses of wine she began to wonder if she'd imagined the undercurrents simmering back at the house.

'You looked a bit tense when I picked

you up.' Steve had obviously tuned into her thoughts.

Hesitating for a moment she decided to take the plunge and perhaps Steve would be able to throw some light on the matter. 'Richard was acting strangely.' It sounded odd now she actually put it into words.

'What kind of strange?'

'Almost as though he didn't want me to go out with you.' She watched his face as she spoke not wanting to run down his friend too much but needing to discuss it with someone. 'He was very sarcastic and well . . . unpleasant, I suppose. It's very difficult to explain.'

Steve sat back abruptly, 'I'm not poaching on his territory am I?'

Her face turned crimson. 'What on earth gives you that idea? We don't even like each other.'

'All right, calm down.' He leaned forward and took her hand across the table. 'It was just a thought, forget it.'

But she didn't want to forget it. 'You must have some reason for thinking there's something between us.'

'He talks a lot about you.'

'Probably saying terrible things.' She tried laughing but it still didn't come out quite right.

'No quite the opposite. He seems to like you a lot and he's always telling me how brilliant you are and how much he admires your efforts to start up in business at your age. In fact I've wondered a couple of times if . . . '

'Absolutely not.' Pulling away her hand she flopped back in her chair not quite believing her own ears. Then she managed to turn the whole episode into a joke, tying to convince Steve just how wrong he was.

She must have succeeded because the next time he spoke it was to ask her to a dinner dance.

'What kind of dance?'

'All boating people really but great fun. I'm sure you'd enjoy it.'

'OK, yes I'd love to come, is it very dressy?'

She barely listened to the reply as for

the rest of the evening the thought of Richard being interested in her was constantly at the back of her mind.

Suddenly she was in the grip of a fierce longing as she wondered what it would be like to be loved by Richard. Surely Steve was wrong. They say a woman always knows and there had been nothing to indicate he wanted any relationship other than that of an employer. But there had been moments when she knew he desired her but desire without any other feeling was empty. Her mind explored the possibilities and then she came down to earth as she remembered the dark, sophisticated woman with the glittering coal eyes. The type of woman he liked was not an inexperienced girl like herself so he certainly wasn't the man for her. Steve was more her type and she set about charming him for the rest of the evening.

Before she left his car, he put a hand behind her head and gently touched her lips with his. Tentatively at first and then gaining confidence he kissed her very thoroughly. Annie sat back and smiled at him, thinking here was a lovely man whose kiss had moved her more than she would have believed it could.

Letting herself in, she walked quietly across the hall barely reaching the stairs before a door opened and Richard stood in his shirtsleeves behind her. His hair was untidy and a thick fair lock fell over one cynically raised eyebrow. 'Was it a good evening?' He had never looked more attractive.

'Yes, thank you,' she stuttered slightly, placing one foot on the first stair. He looked large and powerful and not in a very good mood.

'I want to speak to you.'

'Can it wait until tomorrow?' Something was telling her not to be alone with him that night.

'No it can't.' He stood aside waiting for her to pass him and go through to his study. His look dared her to refuse and reluctantly she turned and preceded him into the room.

'Well what is it you want to talk about?'

'Steve.'

'I beg your pardon?'

'This is exactly the kind of thing I wanted to avoid. I brought you here against my better judgment and I don't want the project jeopardised with any emotional relationships.'

Her eyes snapped up. 'How dare you speak to me like that? What I do out of office hours is my business.'

'On the contrary anything that interferes with your work is my business. I didn't want a young woman for the job. If Galling Computers had been able to send one of their team immediately, you wouldn't be here at all.'

'Well I am here,' her hands clenched and added to her fury. 'There's no question of my getting involved with Steve, we're just friends.'

'Rubbish, there's no such thing.'

'If I was a man and had gone for a drink with Steve to talk about work would that upset you?'

'Of course not, that's different.' He began to look slightly disconcerted.

'It's no different.' She could feel her temper running away. 'Why can't you get rid of those stupid ideas about women?' She glared up at him. 'We had dinner together and what did we talk about?' She moved nearer suppressing an almost irresistible urge to slap his arrogant face. 'We talked about work. Work,' she repeated. 'W-O-R-K,' she spelled the word slowly.

At the mocking, disbelieving expression of his face, her control broke and one arm lifted. It reached her shoulder before he grabbed her wrist, tipping her off balance and dragging her towards him.

'Then he's a fool,' he muttered thickly. 'If I took you to dinner, we wouldn't talk about work.' His head lowered and his other arm came round her. Unable to move she stood like a small animal in a trap.

'What would we do?' she whispered.

His mouth was firm, warm but undemanding as though his kiss was held in check while he gauged her reaction. Then her lips softened and parted slightly and it was evidently the signal he had been waiting for and his kiss deepened. Pulling her even closer his tongue flicked over her lower lip. Her wrap slipped to the floor as his hand left her wrist and stole lightly up her arm, skimming over the fabric of her dress until it reached her exposed neck. A slight sigh of satisfaction escaped him as he found her soft bare skin. Hesitating for just a moment she relaxed and wound her arms around him, her fingers in the fine hair at the nape of his neck.

'Why do you like accountants, isn't my brain good enough for you?'

'What?' She pulled away not believing what she'd heard. He had spoilt it again. He might as well have thrown a bucket of cold water over her.

'Next weekend it will be my turn.'

'Next weekend?'

'I want you to come out on the boat with me.'

'No.'

'Yes, we've both been working hard. Saturday will be a day away.'

She opened her mouth to argue and shut it again. It was far too late to argue so why not just ride things out while she was here? A day out on the boat might be just what she needed, away from the house and the office.

If he wanted to pay her to enjoy herself why should she refuse?

6

She expected that a man who drove a top of the range car would have a top of the range boat and was not disappointed. Early light glinted on the gleaming cruiser. The pure white of its sleek lines was relieved by just a fine deck line stripe of deep blue. It was a beautiful, sleekly styled thoroughbred that yelled money. It was also bigger than she'd imagined and altogether extremely intimidating.

Glancing at him from under her lashes, Annie idly wondered how much he was worth. The charming thatched house, the car and now this boat must add up to serious money. His direct attitude had misled her and she'd never thought of him as a rich man but now supposed he must be.

'It looks very nice,' she muttered the understatement of the year.

'Nice,' he grinned. 'Yes I suppose you could say that.'

Raking her mind for something sensible to say, she tried again. 'You go for the top end of the market judging by your car and now your boat.'

'I buy the best,' he answered briefly. 'After all I feel the boat is a good advertisement for my business.' He gave her the idea that to buy the best was both sensible and logical. It was said without any affectation and she recognised he was not a man to flaunt his possessions. A man who was very much his own person.

'You didn't say where we're going,' she questioned nervously. The boat looked as though it could go half way round the world and back.

'Just over to the Isle of Wight. No distance at all and as I've got some papers to deliver we can combine business with pleasure.'

Following him from the car she was perversely annoyed he hadn't commented on her outfit. Not knowing what she was expected to wear she'd managed to put together what she hoped was suitable for the trip. Her white trainers were teamed with blue shorts and a blue and white top while, in her bag there was a rolled up track suit in case the weather cooled. 'At least I match the boat,' she muttered half under her breath.

'That was the first thing I noticed.'

'Oh,' she replied somewhat inadequately, thinking very sharp hearing could now be added to his list of attributes.

'Especially the shorts,' he cast a long look at the length of exposed leg, 'and for once your hair looks right tied back like that.'

She glared at him and tossed the bunch of hair back over her shoulder.

He helped her as they stepped down into the saloon. Looking at the tastefully appointed accommodation she couldn't keep back a gasp of surprise as she saw the deep blue carpet which covered the whole of the area and contrasted with the oak panelled walls.

Watching her face he was obviously pleased at her reaction, making his whole expression lighter and far less off-putting than usual. In fact in his white slacks and tee shirt he appeared much younger today. Less of the businessman and the shuttered look she dreaded had disappeared altogether. He looked almost boyish and, like a boy, was enjoying showing off his possession.

'Very impressive.' Where do you go? Further than the Isle of Wight!'

'If I have the time, anywhere that I fancy. I go to France frequently, usually down as far as St Malo in Brittany.' He shrugged, sweeping the cabin with his hand. 'All this, I assure you, isn't meant to impress but why not be comfortable and of course I am in the business of boat chandlery.' Suddenly they were in another area. 'Here's the galley, not much room but everything is here, hob, fridge, no oven but there's a microwave. Let's go up again and you can see the cockpit.' Once more he took her hand and continued to hold it when they were on deck. 'You won't fall off,' he teased, watching her worried face, 'there are plenty of guard rails as you can see.'

The cockpit was another surprise, giving an impression of being more of a second lounge with its padded benches and tables.

'There's a canopy that can be fitted quickly in case of bad weather.'

She gazed at the dials and switches with awe. 'Sailing this must be such a huge responsibility.'

'Richard!' A woman hailed them and the spell was broken. His arms dropped as he turned and moved away. With an awful certainty Annie knew it was Pascale. Shading her eyes she recognised the shiny dark head and gulped when she noticed the deceptively simple white designer trousers and shirt which made her own shorts and top look more suitable for a school netball team.

Startled she heard him mutter and knew instinctively he was far from pleased to see the other woman. In fact he was annoyed at the interruption.

Glancing at Annie he squeezed her shoulder. 'I'll just be a moment.'

Annie watched as he stepped lightly off and made his way towards the girl who'd now been joined by an older man. Unashamedly she stared trying to gauge from their greeting the closeness of the relationship. Seeing the dark woman lift her face for his kiss, an almost physical pain stabbed her and she clutched at her middle and turned away. Even though the feeling was unfamiliar she knew what it was, she was ridiculously and stupidly jealous. But why?

'Ready to set off?'

She hadn't heard him return and hoped he hadn't read anything from her face. It would be dreadful if he guessed the line her thoughts were taking. Quickly trying to get herself under control she answered, 'Yes, ready when you are.' She found herself giggling. 'Do I have to call you skipper?'

'This isn't exactly a world cruise.' He laughed, matching her mood. 'Sorry about the delay but Pascale's father wanted a quick word, we often put a bit of business each other's way.'

Nervously she stayed close beside him in the cockpit admiring the sure way he manouvered away from the marina. Then they were heading out to sea and it was exhilarating and exciting and frightening all rolled together.

'Can I do anything?' she asked at last when her breathing was on a more even keel. Then looking up and noticing the way his fair hair was tousled by the wind, it became uneven again. Her glance dropped and there were his hands, tanned and firm with the boat responding to every move.

'We're going to cruise around so you can make some coffee if you like or get a couple of cold drinks from the fridge.' His eyebrow rose again. 'Perhaps then you'd like to sunbathe . . . '

In spite of the fact she'd already decided her place was not going to be in the galley her voice was replying, 'I'll try the coffee.' A few minutes later she knew this normally simple job was extremely complicated on board. Remembering to stand the mugs on a damp cloth to stop them sliding about and also not to fill them to the brim, they still slopped slightly. Finally she grasped them firmly, put them on a tray with some biscuits and carried it triumphantly up on deck.

'Good girl,' his grin and wind blown hair made him look an entirely different person. 'You managed well.' He seemed pleased with her achievement and she revelled in his praise.

Tossing her sun streaked hair she tore away the constricting ribbon and let it blow wildly around her face and shoulders. Her eyes were bright and her soft mouth turned up as, lifting her face to the sun, she was suddenly completely happy. Raising slim arms she brushed her hair from her eyes completely unaware of the man who watched her.

Then remembering she was not alone she turned to find him close beside her. The grey of the sea was reflected in his eyes in which were unfathomable depths of wanting and asking. Annie held his gaze just that second too long. Now she could not look away and her heart began to thud and she was sinking in those grey pools.

His kiss, when it came, sent her swirling to new heights and she was strangely convinced she was drowning but it had nothing to do with the sea.

'The boat . . . ' she stuttered at last, 'no one's steering it.' Her eyes as they looked out to sea were misty and confused.

'It's all taken care of,' he teased. 'This is the age of high technology, you at least should know that.'

With a strength of mind that surprised even her, she managed to disentangle herself from his arms.

The rest of the day passed pleasantly enough. Leaving the boat floating happily in a private marina, a friend's car was put at their disposal.

'I have to drop off these papers for a signature but I'll only be a short while and then we'll have lunch.'

He stopped the car in front of a small shop and reached for his briefcase. 'Won't be long,' he said as he opened the door.

'Okay. I might get out and stretch my legs.'

Instead of going into the shop she watched as he went swiftly up an outside staircase into what she assumed to be an office.

In the meantime the shop window had a good display of sailing clothes and Annie decided to leave the car to take a look.

Attracted by a particularly nice jacket she was inside the shop before she knew it and stood looking at a rack of similar tops while another customer was being served.

'How much longer will it belong to you?' Someone else's conversation drifted over to her.

'Just a matter of hours, my husband is signing the contract today.'

'You must feel dreadful that you're losing your family business.'

'I think now we'll both be glad when it's over. As you know, the threat has been hanging over us for some time and . . . '

Feeling embarrassed she moved away. Was this the reason they were here? Was Richard taking over this shop? The older woman who was serving had a weary and almost resigned air about her.

Suddenly feeling guilty as though she belonged to the enemy camp Annie returned to the car.

Richard came back with a satisfied smile. 'That's business completed and now lunch.' He turned to her. 'Are you hungry?'

He didn't seem to need an answer which was just as well as her head was spinning. Had he just acquired another business from the elderly couple? If so he was more ruthless than she supposed.

She protested briefly that her shorts and top weren't suitable for the elaborate restaurant he chose.

'You won't be the only one casually dressed, you forget we're in the centre of a large boating community. Besides,' he added, 'with those legs you'll be welcome anywhere.'

Of course he was right. No one turned so much as a hair as they entered the restaurant. Tucking her bare legs quickly under the table she caught his amused expression.

'Don't be so inhibited.' Well at least he didn't say *I told you so* which was all to his credit. As she watched him attack his food with enthusiasm she wondered if she was wrong to assume the take-over of the small shop. But it would be better to put it at the back of her mind and try to find out later.

It clouded over on the way back which somewhat spoilt the journey for Annie and she shrugged into the top of her blue tracksuit.

'What do you think of boats and the sea, now?' he asked her hopefully.

'I think I could get quite hooked on this kind of life.' It was said without thinking and suddenly she was embarrassed hoping he didn't think it was a hint for him to take her out again.

'Yes, it's a great life.' He was silent for a few minutes as though relishing the power of the craft slicing through the grey sea. 'It's good to get away from business for a bit and sort of re-charge the batteries.'

Smiling, she nodded in reply.

'By the way,' she caught a slight hesitation in his manner. 'There's a dance Saturday, quite a good affair. Would you come with me, as my partner, I mean?'

She could have sworn he sounded ever so slightly unsure of himself and consequently smiled as she said gently, 'Thank you, but Steve's already asked me and I've promised to go with him.'

An angry flush crossed his cheekbones. 'Oh, think nothing of it, I dare say Pascale will partner me.'

'I'm sorry,' she offered again sensing how much he minded her refusal.

'Don't worry,' he threw the fragile moment away. 'I usually go with her, we understand each other.'

From then on the day was ruined and the air of camaraderie that had developed on the Island abruptly faded. I just bet they understand each other, she thought.

I bet they're two of a kind.

7

Leaving her room next morning she bumped into Katie In fact she had the idea that the girl had been waiting for her.

'Did you enjoy Dad's boat?' There was aggression in her voice. 'I wondered why he took you but I expect he was just being kind.' She didn't look up and meet Annie's eyes.

'Yes,' she answered quickly. 'I'm sure he was.'

'Pascale is his girlfriend you know,' she started to walk ahead and reaching the top of the stairs turned and said, 'I think he'll marry her. Granny and I have talked about it a lot and that's fine with me, she's cool.'

Annie's steps faltered and she couldn't believe what she'd just heard. The child had quite deliberately warned her off. It was unbelievable. Well one thing was for sure, Richard's daughter was very grown up for her age or else Annie was thoroughly out of touch with children. Katie was obviously someone to be reckoned with, just like her father, thought Annie. She didn't know whether to be amused or annoyed. But the thing that hurt was the idea that Katie didn't like her. But why was that such a surprise, when the girl had gone out of her way to avoid her ever since she'd arrived.

Also she was becoming increasingly uneasy with Richard. He appeared to be attracted to her but just where did he think that would lead? More importantly, was he happy with the work she was doing? He hadn't said anything specific but there had been a few worrying hints dropped and of course the comment from Pascale. Was she reading too much into them? Surely a businessman such as Richard wouldn't keep her in his employment just because he was physically attracted to her?

Perhaps she could get in touch with Mark and prime him to telephone to say that something in the office required her immediate attention. Pleased with this brilliant idea she grabbed keys, brief-case and handbag and ran lightly down the stairs. When she was half out of the front door she risked calling a casual goodbye and dashed to her car. She just had to get to the office first so she could telephone in private.

All went well. The journey was completed in record time and the cleaner was still there to let her in. Running through the general office she pushed open her door, threw everything onto her desk and snatched the receiver. It was then that her luck ran out. Mark was not at home and the only reply was the frustrating burr of the answering machine.

'Starting work early?' Why did he always look so big framed in a doorway and why this habit of creeping up on her?

'Of course,' she lied, opening her top

drawer and wedging in her bag. 'I've a particularly busy day ahead. After all the sooner I have it all tied up, the sooner I can get back to my own business and my next job.'

Ignoring her excuses, he continued, 'As you made such a quick getaway this morning, I wondered if you were up to something.' Pierced with glinting eyes that gave the worrying impression they were looking into her soul, she faced him bravely.

'Whatever gives you that idea,' she tried a light laugh, which came out like more of a breathless giggle and did nothing at all for the image she was trying to portray.

With a complete change of subject he said, 'We'll all be going to the dance together this weekend. You and I and Steve and Pascale.'

It was noticeable how the pairing had changed even though she was officially going with Steve. Oh well, she'd just have to put a brave face on the whole episode and buy something stunning to wear. She would leave early today, perhaps take most of the afternoon off and drive straight to Southampton.

'I'm leaving early today,' she said quickly.

'Why?' Thick brows drew across in a deep frown, 'Meeting someone perhaps?' There was sharp steel in his voice but for the life of her Annie simply couldn't understand what he might be feeling to make it like that.

'If you must know I'm going shopping.'

'Shopping? But we don't need anything. Mother looks after that.'

'Not that kind of shopping,' she sighed in exasperation. 'Something personal for myself.'

Slowly he grasped what she was saying. 'Oh clothes,' he dismissed airily. 'You can get those in your own time. There's work to do here today.' His attention shifted to the papers on her desk as though that was the end of the matter.

'No,' she stood her ground. 'I want

an outfit for the dance, unless of course,' she added sarcastically, 'you'd rather I dashed back to London to collect a dress from my flat? Although frankly I think Southampton would be quicker.' With her blue eyes flashing she waited for his answer.

'Oh you want to make Steve sit up and take notice?' He subsided into a chair and lolling back in it, with hands clasped clasping behind his head, regarded her steadily.

Watching the chair balancing precariously on its two legs she had trouble resisting the urge to give a hefty shove and send him sprawling backwards. But managed to swing round on her heel and leave the room.

* ★ ★

As she dressed the following Saturday she admitted her new outfit was worth every penny of the extravagant price. A dream of a dress, black and deceptively simple on the hanger but once she slipped it over her head the superb cut caused the fine silky fabric to cling and flow in all the right places. Demure long sleeves contrasted with the daring plunge neckline while the bodice hugged her so well that a bra would have spoilt the line. Smoothing the skirt over her hips she watched it swirl and flare around her calves. It was more than satisfactory.

Smugly deciding that black suited her dark blonde hair she placed gold hoops in her ears and stood back to admire the effect. It was terrific, so unlike her usual work-a-day self that she barely stifled a giggle.

As Annie came slowly down the stairs Richard and Steve were standing together in the hall and she delighted in the shocked expression on each of their faces. 'Will I do?' She even plucked up courage to twirl around.

'You look marvellous,' Steve was the only one to speak. 'You'll be the belle of the ball,' he continued with rather old world charm.

Stupidly hurt that he hadn't admired her appearance she looked at Richard. But the only sign of emotion on his face was bad temper and she wondered at the evening ahead which seemed to be off to a bad start.

She bore the scrutiny of Pascale who looked her up and down, also obviously surprised by her appearance but, unlike the men, her glance was cold and disapproving. 'I often wonder if blondes should wear black.' She said it with just the right degree of hesitation so as not to appear offensive. She looked down at her own deep wine dress, clinging like a second skin and showing even more cleavage than Annie. 'Perhaps something brighter would suit you better. You really must come to my boutique one day,' she added in a deceptively friendly fashion.

'Oh I reckon Annie looks great in black.' Steve was quick to her defence.

'Yes, very sexy,' drawled Richard which earned Annie a further look of bitterness from the girl's dark eyes.

Eventually they were settled at a table and Richard quite unexpectedly called for champagne. Lifting his glass he said, 'Here's to us all, or should I say welcome Annie to the boating fraternity.'

Smiling with shy pleasure she momentarily met warmth in his eyes. The throw away speech didn't actually toast her but it was near enough for her to be aware of another quelling glance from Pascale. The woman touched Richard's arm with a familiar manner as she asked him to dance.

'Come on,' Steve was reaching for her hand. 'Let's join them.'

Steve was a surprisingly good dancer, light on his feet and his usual quiet manner seemed to take a back seat. He led her with more enthusiasm than technical ability but she loved every moment of it and followed him almost with abandon, knowing she was safe with Steve. He was a lovely man and deserved her attention.

Her mood lightened as they made

their way back to the table. It was going to be a good evening. All she must do was concentrate on Steve and forget about Richard. Pascale managed to ignore her and eventually Annie gave up trying to engage her in any kind of friendly conversation. Wondering why the other girl was so difficult to be with she didn't notice Richard standing up.

'Annie,' he held out his hand. She couldn't ignore it without causing a scene and she followed him meekly to the floor. He had captured her without her being aware of it and pulled her firmly to him and then even closer and it was then that she stepped completely out of character and allowed her arms to snake up around his neck. His quick intake of breath was audible as he pulled her more closely to him.

Was it her imagination or were the lights lower?

Well if the lights were low and no one could see, it wouldn't matter if she touched the back of his neck with her fingers and allowed them to reach up to the soft fair hair. Her breath left her in a small sigh of pure pleasure. All thoughts of concentrating on Steve had fled. There was only Richard and her, dancing in the dark. The feel of his body so near to her was the most wonderful sensation she'd ever known.

Now she knew what people meant when they said they wished a moment would go on forever for that was what she was wishing now. How lonely it would be when the moment ended and the music finally stopped.

And then what she'd been dreading happened. The music stopped, the lights were bright and Annie rubbed her eyes as if waking from a dream.

He seemed to know how her knees trembled because his arm around her was firm and supportive on the way back to the other couple.

She couldn't remember the rest of the evening. It passed in front of her and there seemed to be no part for her to take. She assumed she spoke and made the right responses because everyone treated her normally. But there was this odd feeling of being unaware of what was happening.

At the end of the evening it was arranged that they drop off Pascale first. 'But it is so early and you are all being so dull,' the girl grumbled sulkily.

'It's one o'clock.' Richard checked the slim gold watch on his tanned wrist. 'Time for your beauty sleep.'

'You haven't always thought like that.' She flashed a suggestive gleam from stormy dark eyes and although he flushed he also recovered quickly.

When they arrived back at the house, Steve collected his car and refused a coffee and Annie and Richard stood in the doorway like an old married couple and watched him drive away. Richard put his arm around her as they walked into the house together and the moment she'd been waiting for arrived. But suddenly, for her, the spell was broken as she remembered the little exchange between him and Pascale. It had ruined it for her.

Grabbing her chin, he forced her to look at him. 'Don't kid me any longer that you're an icy business woman with a computer for a heart. Under those prissy clothes and the tied back hair you're fire and warmth.'

Pushing away his hand she snapped, 'I should never have come here, I should have gone to a hotel. This . . . this ridiculous arrangement isn't working. I don't know why you suggested it.'

'Don't you, don't you really?' He drawled. 'Not very perceptive are you?' Then looking at her puzzled face he seemed to relent, 'I'll tell you one day, unless,' he moved closer, 'you find out for yourself.'

Twisting away she ran up the stairs, terrified he would pursue her.

Her room was a sanctuary and she flung herself on the bed hating what was happening to her. Clutching the pillow she tried to bite back the tears that refused to obey and flowed freely down her cheeks and wept desperately, unable to come to terms with her changing attitudes. Always she'd despised women who relied on men for their happiness.

She had everything she'd always wanted. An apartment of her own, thanks to the generosity of her parents who understood her need to stand on her own two feet. Her business wasn't exactly booming but it was building up nicely and this current job would help a lot. Treasured above all she had her independence and couldn't allow this to be taken away by such a self centered man. She'd fight her feelings for him every inch of the way.

8

When she awoke her normal sense of well being was short lived. Sitting up and swinging her legs to the floor, a hot tide of embarrassment rushed through her as she remembered the dance.

The music and general atmosphere had a lot to answer for, a barely lit room, clasped in someone's arms and a haunting, throbbing tune was enough to send anyone over the edge.

Maybe she should try to get them back onto a more friendly footing and dressing quickly she ran down stairs to find Katie on the way to the pool.

'Gran's out until teatime,' the girl said briskly without even wishing Annie good morning.

Impetuously Annie ventured, 'If you're going for a swim perhaps I could come with you?'

'No thank you,' Katie tossed her

head. 'I'm swimming seriously.'

Her own appetite for breakfast swiftly vanished and looking around the luxury kitchen she knew what she'd do. She'd cook lunch and if Richard came in perhaps he'd accept it for the peace offering it was intended and if not, well, she would enjoy it herself even if she choked on every mouthful.

Cleaning and cutting vegetables into tiny strips she brooded over the moment when she'd have to face him and worried about the best way to handle it.

Trying to concentrate on the job in hand she wondered if he and Katie would find her style of cooking to their liking. Laura usually cooked a traditional Sunday roast but given the choice Annie would opt for lots of vegetables rather than meat. Reaching for the spices, she placed them near to hand while wondering if a stir-fry would be to their taste. Well, she glanced through the window, it looked as though they were in for a hot day and a light meal would not only be better but could also be cooked in a few minutes. She even decided to prepare the rice to accompany the meal now and then it could be re-heated in the microwave.

There was something very therapeutic about cooking, at least there was here in this lovely kitchen. Gazing through the window again she decided the view had a lot to do with the pleasure in preparing the simple meal. Annie didn't find cooking in her apartment as enjoyable and satisfying as this. Picking up the saucepan of rice in one hand and a strainer in the other, an awful thought occurred to her. It couldn't be because she was cooking for someone else, could it, and that the someone else was a man? Furiously she tipped the rice into the sieve and ran the cold tap over it while she wrestled with the thought. Surely she of all people didn't hanker to be the little woman happily preparing food for her man.

'Rubbish,' she said indignantly out loud. I'm a career woman and in any case, she thought, Richard wasn't her man, he wasn't anyone's man and probably never would be.

★ ★ ★

Later, sitting in the garden drinking a fruit juice she heard the car. Clutching the glass she listened to the expensive clunk of the door and heard his quick footsteps coming through the kitchen. Now that the moment was here she wanted to run and clung to the glass as if it were an anchor. If the glass was put down on the garden table she would be up and running through the gate into the forest.

Instinctively she sank lower into the padded chair trying to make herself smaller and hoping he would perhaps think she was out.

'I see you've started lunch.' Suddenly he was in front of her and his voice was friendly and casual.

'It's just a stir fry, I hope that's okay.' Could that really be her replying in an equally casual manner while inside she was churning away.

Hesitating for a moment, as though he too was feeling the strain, he shrugged. 'I'll find some wine.' Then just as she would have sprung up, 'Finish your drink, there's no hurry. Where's Katie?'

'She said something about homework. I think she's in her room.' The girl seemed to have gone out of her way to avoid Annie, which was hurtful.

Taking a large swallow of the cold liquid. Annie felt as never before the need for caffeine and wished she'd chosen coffee instead. Lying back in the chair she tried to relax and get herself together by taking deep breaths and telling her muscles to unlock.

Not only had he found the wine but also when she went in had laid the dining room table with three places. Gulping, she couldn't take her gaze away. It looked so intimate, too intimate, and Annie was only glad it was the middle of the day and not the evening, which would have given the situation a strange air of romance.

Relieved that all the ingredients were ready she heated some oil and threw in the vegetables. If he had watched her preparations she thought wryly, she would have probably cut off her finger.

'Anything I can do?' He was hovering so terribly near.

'No, really, it'll be ready in a moment.' Swallowing nervously she asked, 'Would you have preferred a roast?' Was that her voice asking the question? She hardly knew what she was saying and it would serve her right if he admitted to being a traditional Sunday lunch person. What would she do then, thaw out a joint and start over again?

'No, this is a favourite of mine. I often make it at weekends. Quick and healthy,' he said with a grin.

'Good heavens, can you cook?' she asked startled by his admission.

'It's an alternative to starving,' he smiled. 'Perhaps I'm not quite the chauvinist you think I am.'

'Of course I don't think that,' she caught his grin and smiled back. 'Yes I do, I think you're the worst I've ever met.'

'Have you ever considered you could be wrong about me?'

The mixture sizzled sending up a spicy warmth. 'What do you mean?'

'You've got me cast in a particular mould of your own imagining.' He sniffed appreciatively. 'Perhaps it's the wrong mould.'

'Oh,' it was so inadequate but what on earth could she say? There was too much to think about. 'Well, let's say you certainly are not the easiest person to get on with.' She stirred vigorously. 'Unless we just rub each other up the wrong way.'

'Perhaps you make me act the part you've cast me in and of course you are delightful to tease.'

This admission seemed to clear the

air and after two glasses of wine and his seemingly sincere compliments on her cooking, she wondered why she'd dreaded seeing him quite so much. Even Katie cleared her plate and muttered her favourite phrase, 'That was cool.' The slight praise from the girl cheered Annie up considerably. She wasn't used to being cold shouldered by someone like Katie.

'This is awfully good,' he helped himself to another portion and she was warmed with happiness that he so obviously enjoyed her meal. 'Do you like cooking?' He smiled and once more she was lost. Tiny lines crinkled around his mouth and lit his eyes and suddenly it would have been nice to have told him that she was a Cordon Bleu cook or something equally as grand.

Poised with her fork in mid air she gasped, realising the precarious line her mind was taking. Did she want him to love her? Of course not, the whole idea was ridiculous.

'Are you okay?' He was looking at

her, concerned. 'Did something go down the wrong way?'

'What?' she answered vaguely and then pulled herself together. 'Yes that's it,' her smile was wide, 'Something went down the wrong way.'

After that the meal progressed leisurely as they talked generally both skirting and avoiding issues, which were uppermost in their minds. Finishing with cheese and fruit she silently complimented herself on a successful lunch and also on handling matters in such a modern manner.

Katie suddenly announced, 'Lucy's coming over and I want to finish my work.' Then she left the room and the atmosphere changed.

'Coffee, perhaps?' He rose from the table. 'I make very good coffee.'

'Oh, em . . . yes please.'

She heard noises from the kitchen and wondered if perhaps what he'd said was true. Was he acting the role she'd cast him in?

'Delicious.' The hot brew smelt

wonderful. 'Of course I keep forgetting that Laura doesn't usually live here and you are obviously used to doing things for yourself.'

'Mother likes her independence and loves having Katie. If she were lonely I would ask her to stay permanently. But she has her own friends and interests, which of course is good for her.'

'Yes, she strikes me as a very balanced person, although I think she's enjoying looking after you at the moment.'

'Most probably,' he laughed. 'This arrangement suits us very well. She is independent but near enough for me to keep an eye on her.'

A pleasant lunch with ordinary, friendly conversation Annie thought as they cleared the table together. Everything straightforward without double edged comments and sexist remarks. But was it going to last?

They were both in the kitchen when the atmosphere suddenly changed. Straightening up from loading the dishwasher she backed into him.

Immediately his hands were on her upper arms and she stood motionless as sensation after sensation throbbed through her body, which trembled as he turned her round to face him.

'I should have let you go to a hotel,' he said slowly, searching her face with his eyes.

'Why didn't you?' she asked. 'You said it was convenient for work.'

'I wanted you here because you were a challenge I couldn't resist and still can't resist. I've never wanted a woman as much as I want you.'

Then she did shrug off those arms. 'Pascale . . . I suppose you want her as well?' she said bitterly.

For a second he looked surprised. 'Yes, I should explain about Pascale.'

'Perhaps you'd better.'

'There was something between us once but it's over now.'

'Does she know that?' she said sarcastically. 'She still seems to think she owns you. You're certainly very close.'

His eyes were true and steady. 'It's

over. I give you my word.' He hesitated. 'I'm doing business with her father at the moment which means I have to see them on a fairly friendly footing. But whatever was between us is in the past and she knows it's finished.'

'Did you love her?'

He smiled. 'It wasn't that kind of relationship. Pascale knows the score, always did.' Drawing her towards him, he held her close. 'Let's forget her.'

'I don't know that I can. I'm sure she wants you back.'

'Only because she now senses that my interests are taken up elsewhere. It was ended on an entirely mutual basis, I can assure you,' he said.

Her expression cleared as she knew that was the sort of reaction to be expected from the other girl.

'Now, where were we?'

Smiling she relaxed in his arms. 'You were telling me why you wanted me to stay here.' She added impishly, 'But you asked your mother here as chaperone as well.'

His fingers were on her neck touching the long strands of hair. 'You wouldn't have stayed if I hadn't.'

'No,' she said simply. 'I wouldn't and perhaps I really shouldn't have.'

Annie made a small, hesitant movement towards him and heard his sigh of satisfaction. She was lost in the deepness of his eyes, trapped by his obvious desire and her emotions were spinning out of control and it was too much to handle, too much to cope with and too unexpected.

So she ran.

Almost falling through the gate she was soon out into the forest and amongst the ponies as they grazed contentedly in the afternoon sun. Coming upon a clearing she threw herself onto the grass. She'd stay here until Laura returned, and it was there, in the warm and peace of the forest that she admitted to herself that she loved him.

9

Crawling from bed after the first weak light of morning appeared Annie was appalled at the dark smudges under her eyes and the way her hair hung like seaweed around her shoulders. Knowing that sleep had never been further away she dragged on the black bikini, crept downstairs and, letting herself through the back door, made for the pool.

As she lowered her body into the cool, gentle water it lapped against her warm flesh. Her brain whirred like a movie film playing back yesterday's scenes. Firmly thrusting away the images she struck out in her beginner's version of the crawl. At least she'd achieved something here, she told herself grimly, she'd mastered her fear of the water and could now swim.

Every thought and idea in her head

always brought her back to him and lying on her back let her mind drift over the previous day. What a complete and utter fool! The signs were there big, bold and clear and yet she hadn't seen them. It was love. All her joy in preparing a meal, of working in his kitchen, being in his house, was so obvious. So obvious that she'd completely missed it.

Annie was so deeply immersed in her thoughts that she only vaguely noticed a slight rocking as a disturbance in the water sent waves gently rolling in her direction. Then as one lapped over her face, it registered and panic struck as she lifted her head and let her feet glide to the bottom. Who or what was in the pool with her?

Close by a sleek, dark-blond head surfaced and they stood as motionless as two statues softly lit with the rays of morning. He cradled her wet body against him and smiled tenderly down, a slightly tentative smile that made him look boyish and a trifle unsure of himself.

'I want you to stay with me.'

'Stay,' she repeated. That wasn't quite what she wanted to hear.

'Yes stay here,' he repeated slowly as though she couldn't understand. 'In this house with me. You like the forest and the countryside, I know you do.' He grinned. 'You'd even get to like the boat, I'm sure.' Then carrying the joke even further, 'And it would do wonders for your swimming.'

Ignoring his humour she tried to encourage him to make a commitment. 'For how long?' she asked bluntly.

'Why worry about that?' He frowned. 'I just know I want us to be together.' His expression cleared and his eyes lit up. 'We'd be good together, you know that as well as me and you'd fit into the life down here.'

As she didn't answer he put her slightly away from him, and continued. 'I know, I expect you think it would be dull after London?' Confused at her silence, he went on. 'It isn't dull at all, it's a pretty good life. The country, the sea, and socially it's got everything and,' he hesitated, 'London isn't so far if you want to go back now and again.'

'I don't hanker after London. I love it here, you know that.'

'Then what is it? He asked with impatience. 'What's stopping you?'

'What about my business?' At that moment it didn't seem very important but she had to keep him talking. She had to give him every opportunity to say the words she was longing to hear.

'Oh, give it up,' he dismissed her ambitions as if they were of no consequence. 'You can work for me. I can do with someone permanently to oversee the computer operation here and in other areas.' He beamed at her as though the problem was easily solved. 'You'd be perfect for the job.'

Was he actually suggesting she give up everything or was she not hearing correctly? 'Work for you?' she challenged, her mood changing rapidly at his insensitive words.

'Of course,' he hugged her to him.

'It's the ideal solution.'

'It might be for you but it certainly isn't for me.' Pulling stiffly away, at that moment her love for him froze and she hated him, hated the indulgent tone of his voice, his casual brushing aside of everything she was trying to build. 'I don't want to work for you. What about my business, my ambitions, my apartment?' she said coldly, trying to keep a rein on her temper.

'You won't need all that if you stay with me.' His head lowered to catch her lips. 'There is everything you need here.'

Trying to hold her emotions together she knew he hadn't got love and marriage on his mind. Why was she so surprised, hadn't this been his style since the first time they met? She didn't even feel anger, just resignation.

'How dare you suggest I give up everything to stay here with you!' she said coldly. It was all over and edging back she came up against the side of the pool, which dug painfully into the top of her shoulders. 'What about your business? Would you give it up to come and live in my apartment?'

'Don't be silly darling,' he was deliberately trying to soothe her. 'That's not the same thing at all. Look at the money I'm making, how could I let it go and what would you expect me to do? Start again in London when everything I've built is here?' Again he smiled in that irritatingly indulgent fashion. 'What a foolish idea.'

'But you expect me to give up everything.'

'It's different.'

'It's just the same,' she whispered. 'You don't understand at all.'

'I don't understand why you want to cling to your business when you could work for me. I'll pay you well,' he added. 'If you're worried about the money aspect.'

'Yes, I expect you would.' She forced the sounds through lips that were rigid with hurt pride. 'That's not what I want.'

'What do you want?' he exploded. 'Tell me and I'll give it to you!'

It pushed her over the edge. 'No, that's not what I want.' In her fury she pummelled his chest with her fists. 'Do you really think you can buy me?'

This was the finish, his very mention of money had killed everything. He only wanted her to live with him — and for how long? Until he tired of her and found another Pascale and then what would she have? She knew what she would have. The embarrassment of working for an ex-lover and with her own business gone beyond recall. No, no, no, she told herself. That was not for her . . . maybe if he'd asked her to marry him . . . Quickly she shrugged the thought away. He hadn't and that was all there was to it.

He was perfectly still, seemingly unaware of the tattoo she was beating on him. 'You don't want to stay?'

There was nothing more she could say without telling him she was old fashioned enough to want to be married. Momentarily she hesitated, on the brink of taking back everything. She was a modern girl so why hold out for marriage? She loved him and he said he loved her but it wasn't only his lack of commitment, but his attitude to her business that made her dig in her heels. If he understood she couldn't give it up, she might agree to live with him but he was asking too much.

'I'm cold,' she said knowing her dream was over. 'I'll get dressed and start my working day.'

He stood back, watching her go, his expression bewildered and unsure.

Later when their eyes met across the table she knew he was waiting for her to say she was leaving and although tempted wouldn't give him the satisfaction. She'd stay and finish the job because it looked as though work was all there would be in the future.

'I'm going away for a bit.' They were alone at the table and his voice broke the heavy silence and she looked across at him surprised. 'I think a break away from each other would be the best thing. Perhaps when I come back you'll have thought things over and be more sensible.'

Seething with anger she bit her lip and looked woodenly at him. 'I doubt it.' Scraping back her chair she rose. 'I'll get into the office early, there's a lot to do.' He didn't offer her a lift or even answer.

So that's how it's going to be, she fumed, he's acting like a spoilt child who can't get his own way. Or perhaps, like her, he was just so angry he could hardly speak. Allowing herself one last look at his face, she managed to say casually, 'Perhaps I'll see you there.'

Stumbling up the stairs through her tears she knew that after he left on this trip she wouldn't see him again. If she worked all the hours she could, the job would be finished before he returned.

Several times he tried to catch her attention at the office but there was always the urgent telephone call to be made or a run on the computer that called for her complete concentration. Nevertheless as she juggled her way through the hours the strain began to tell, making her nervous and irritable. Sensing he was anxious to talk, she shut herself away in her own private shell. Tough and unapproachable and if there was an unhappy and bewildered look in his eyes, it was ignored.

Her one trump card was that her work was nearly completed and this knowledge was kept from him

Then he went away and, expecting to feel better once his overpowering presence was removed, she at once plunged into deep depression. She'd hoped the cloud of strain hovering overhead would suddenly grow a silver lining or disappear entirely. It didn't happen. The cloud was still above but it was a symbol of emptiness that sapped her enthusiasm and chipped away at her ambition. She drifted along living in his house and wishing that he were still there.

The telephone call from Pascale was

the last straw that drove her to work even harder in a desperate attempt to complete it as soon as possible.

She'd just instructed the computer to print when the 'phone rang. Absently she picked it up, her eyes still on the screen.

'Annie?' With sinking heart she registered the soft tones of Pascale.

'Yes,' she answered abruptly.

'Are you coming to my boutique?'

'Maybe but I'm busy at the moment.' Nothing on earth would make her set foot in the other girl's shop and have her criticise her taste in clothes.

'I thought I'd tell you that I am off to France today so if you want my personal attention you'll have to wait until I get back.'

There was a subtle underlying reason for the call. There was something the girl was trying to tell her without actually putting it into words. They weren't friends and so the conversation was pointless. Annie shrugged, just wanting to get her off the 'phone. 'I may not have time,' she said, trying to be polite. 'I will be leaving for home very shortly.'

'Oh of course, I know the job hasn't worked out well for you,' the slight breathy laugh grated on Annie's nerves. 'How very unfortunate. Does Richard know or shall I tell him when I see him?' The voice was satisfied and dripped like syrup.

Richard?' This was the reason for the call.

'Of course, he is also in France but perhaps you don't know.'

The receiver clicked as the point of the call was made. 'Bitch,' hissed Annie under her breath. 'The utter bitch.' She glared at the telephone as though it was responsible for her fury. Come to her boutique indeed, all she wanted was to tell me she'd be seeing Richard in France.

So that's where he was. Not wanting to appear too interested, she hadn't bothered to ask and now it had boomeranged and put her at a disadvantage Laura

154

had mentioned he'd taken the boat so he could very well be seeing Pascale and imagining seeing them together made her head start to throb.

How quickly he'd turned to Pascale, she thought bitterly. While she relived every touch and word of the weekend of the dance, he'd put it out of his mind as though of no importance. He said he wanted her and asked her to stay with him, to live with him but when she refused had quickly focused his attention on another woman. How it hurt, picturing them together in her mind's eye but even through the hurt she realised more than ever that her decision was the right one, in fact the only one.

That evening when she drew up she sat for several moments studying the house and wondered if she was a fool to turn down the chance of living in it on the semi permanent basis he suggested. The sun picked out the dark beams, stark against the white wash on the walls and fell on the great bronze fittings on the heavy door. It was a beautiful home but it wasn't for her and she'd better hang on to that thought.

'Where exactly is Richard?' Annie asked during the evening meal, trying to achieve just the right degree of interest in her voice.

'Didn't he tell you dear? He went to the Isle of Wight but now he is on his way to France.'

'France,' she echoed weakly, automatically filling her fork with salad.

'He's very fond of France and of course has business interests there which he's hoping to expand. Very European isn't it?' She gave a little giggle. 'He even speaks the language quite fluently but then whatever he does he does well.' She studied Annie. 'You look a bit peaky dear, it's just as well you were in early tonight. You should get Richard to take you across the channel next time you go sailing. There's nothing quite like a sea breeze to blow away the cobwebs.'

Somehow she got through the meal.

The air was still and heavy and after helping to clear away she let herself through the forest gate and strolled moodily around.

So it was true, he was with Pascale who had again intimated that he wasn't satisfied with her work. Should she believe the other girl or wait and see what happened.

Approaching a group of ponies she watched them quietly grazing and stood for some time looking at one in particular pulling at the gorse. Damn the man, he was even right about the forest. She did love it and wouldn't hesitate to swap her town environment for the peace and serenity around her. In the right circumstances, of course.

Reluctantly she re-traced her steps, feeling slightly better and decided watching animals must be quite therapeutic. After all, she wasn't the only one who'd ever suffered unrequited love and here she was acting like a heroine from the Middle Ages. Walking more briskly and thinking once again that if she wanted to survive she'd have to pull herself together. The only problem was putting Richard from her mind. To erase every word, every touch, and forget about his kisses and his smile. That's all, nothing to it really, it should be easy.

★   ★   ★

Returning to the house in a slightly calmer frame of mind she resolved to keep her sights firmly fixed on future goals and think positive. It must have worked because as she entered the sitting room Laura glanced up from the television programme she was watching and said, 'Steve rang for you dear, I told him you'd ring him back.'

'Oh thanks,' she answered and smiled as Laura returned quickly to what was obviously one of her favourite programmes. Steve, he was the very person she needed to take her mind off Richard and her problems.

She would ask him out like the

modern liberated woman she was trying to become and, dialling his number, thought over what had happened since they'd last met at that fateful dance. Guiltily, she was also aware he hadn't so much as entered her head.

He sounded just the same, which was surprising as she was certain she was an entirely different person. As it was, Annie didn't need to ask him out.

'Annie, do you fancy coming out with me for a drink and a meal tomorrow evening?' When she didn't immediately reply he continued, 'I take it that you are still available?'

'What a quaint expression,' she hoped her laugh sounded genuine. 'Of course I'm available, what on earth made you say that?' Immediately wishing she hadn't asked the question she wondered if she was embarrassing him.

'Oh, it was just a feeling I had about Richard but obviously I was wrong so perhaps we could still meet each other?'

Just a feeling, how right you were

Steve, she thought grimly. And then straightened up and said all the right things including how much she was looking forward to seeing him which was quite true but not for the reasons he was obviously hoping.

She deliberately told Laura she was going out with Steve and managed to sound quite excited. Trusting her enthusiasm wasn't out of proportion with the date, she hoped if Richard telephoned his mother she'd let him know that Annie was happy and dating another man. Pleased with her performance and to add to the illusion, she told Laura she'd go to Southampton again first thing tomorrow to buy something new.

The dress was straight cut, the fabric of the skirt heavy with a slight slit at the side. Tightly belted and sleeveless it both hugged and concealed her upper body in a most alluring way while the deep blue gave depth and mystery to her eyes. Faint guilt feelings about Steve stirred again as she decided to look her best for him. In the back of her mind she felt she'd behaved badly on Saturday and even if he hadn't seen the sensuous way she and Richard had danced, she was all too aware of it herself.

It was worth the new dress just to see the effect it had on him as she opened the door. 'Wow, that's a knockout!' he said and as she invited him in she was reminded of the last time she had gone out with him.

While he chatted with Laura, Annie went to her room and flew around gathering up her bag and coat and while she was walking down the stairs the telephone rang. Calling out 'I'll get it,' she reached the hall and picked up the receiver.

The line crackled slightly then Richard's voice was as clear as if he were standing next to her. 'Annie, is that you?'

'Hello Richard.' She tried to make her voice flat and calm while inwardly she was trembling.

'Will you tell Mother I'll be home next week and, Annie, we have to talk, if you could . . . ?'

'I'll fetch Laura and you can tell her yourself.'

'But Annie I want to talk to you . . . '

'Sorry,' she said deliberately, 'I'm just on my way out with Steve.'

'There was a heavy silence for a moment before she gently laid down the telephone and called out to Laura to come to the telephone.

Trust him to call at this moment and spoil my evening. He couldn't have timed it better if he tried. 'You hateful thing,' she said to the inoffensive instrument and Laura glanced at her questioningly as she came into the hall.

Steve was quiet as they drove and glancing at him, Annie was worried by the determined set of his jaw. However, once they were seated he relaxed as they ordered their food but she knew deep inside, he was going to mention the night of the dance.

He cleared his throat and started in

abruptly, 'I couldn't help noticing the way Richard took over last Saturday.' He reached for her hand and not wanting to hurt him, she let him clasp her fingers. 'I noticed the way he looked at you.'

There was a question in his voice and she chose her words carefully. 'Richard is a man who is used to getting what he wants.' She hesitated, 'We just don't want the same things.' Then, biting her lip, continued quickly as though once the words were out she'd feel better. 'That's all there is to it,' and she smiled brightly.

For a time his expression was puzzled but at last bewilderment gave way to understanding as he worked out what she was trying to say. 'He's a good man Annie, even though he's tough on women.'

'It isn't important,' she said brightly changing the subject. 'I've nearly finished here and I'll be moving back to London in a couple of days.'

'Can we still see each other? I often

drive down to visit a couple of clients.'
He waited for her answer and when she
didn't reply asked, 'Is there anyone
else?'

Again she was silent wishing the
conversation hadn't taken this turn.

'It's Richard,' he said. 'I've been a
fool to think it was all on his side.'

Mutely she nodded.

'You mustn't let yourself believe he's
the only one who can make you happy,'
he said earnestly. 'There's probably two
or three men who'd fit the bill —
including me,' he finished with a grin.

'Probably,' Annie muttered wanting
the subject to end.

Oh hell, this wasn't going the way
she'd planned. This evening she'd
wanted to shelve all emotional involve-
ments and enjoy herself and instead
Steve was pushing her into a corner.

'So, what do you think? Can we see
each other once you've left here?'

'If you visit I'll always be pleased to
see you,' she looked at him honestly, 'as
a friend.'

'As a friend,' he agreed, looking not the slightest put out. Steve was a nice, friendly bear of a man and she knew his emotions would never run deeply like her own. He would amble happily through life, content with his lot but he was a good, kind man who she'd like to see again.

For her, the evening never really got off the ground. They talked and laughed and the food was superb but always she knew Richard was somewhere between them stopping her from enjoying a casual evening out.

Arriving back Annie was relieved to find that Laura hadn't waited up and, feeling absolutely drained, she slowly climbed the winding stairs.

Everything was wrong, she decided, dragging a cotton nightdress over her head. Steve's rather obscure hint that he'd like to be more than a friend had spoiled the outing and far from lightening her mood had made her more depressed than ever.

Men, she fumed, trying to get

comfortable, they're so difficult. Steve, she knew, would be like putty in her hands but she didn't want him. She wanted Richard who seemed to get along just fine without her.

Why couldn't the people we love, love us in return, were her last thoughts before she dropped off to sleep.

10

'Would you pick up Katie?' Laura asked. 'Of course,' Annie agreed and, armed with Lucy's address, she set out in her own car.

When she collected her, the girl was unusually quiet, 'Are you okay Katie?' she asked.

'It's Lucy,' her voice broke. 'She doesn't want to be my friend anymore.' Tears started to roll down her face.

Annie stopped the car in the first clearing she saw and without hesitation took the young girl in her arms. Surprisingly Katie didn't pull away but continued to cry silently.

'She doesn't mean it, you know, Katie.' She stroked the long fair hair from the child's forehead. 'By tomorrow she'll have changed her mind.'

'Pascale says you shouldn't let friends mess you around. I told Lucy that and she said she didn't care.'

Annie recalled the heartache of her own school days when friends were unkind. 'Just hang on in there Katie. Do you still want Lucy as your friend?'

'Yes,' the girl jerked back her head and her grey eyes flashed.

'Then hang on and it'll sort itself out. We're all different and we have to accept our friends as they are, even the bits we don't like. Maybe it's not worth being bad friends just because she sometimes messes you around.'

'I don't mind really. I'd rather put up with that than not be her friend even though Pascale . . . ' Her voice trailed off and Annie hugged the girl to her, seeing not her usual self-possession but her childlike vulnerability.

'This is all part of growing up Katie,' she said kindly. 'It happens to us all and you have to accept the rough with the smooth. Just try not to worry.'

'You reckon it'll be okay tomorrow?'

'I'd take bets on it.'

'You're cool, Annie,' the girl murmured and Annie felt delightfully warm and happy. At last she'd seen the real Katie, and it was the break through she'd been hoping for but now it was too late to build a good relationship and suddenly she was overwhelmed with sadness.

Driving herself to work the last morning, Annie slowed through the forest, noting the subtle changes that had taken place since her arrival. Everything was lush and in full bloom, even the ponies which had been born in May, no longer tottered on their spindly legs but were now sturdy although they still kept very close to their mothers' sides.

She remembered Richard explaining that each season had it's own beauty. In her mind she could almost hear him saying that when autumn came and the leaves changed colour and fell she might still be here. Sadly she knew that it was only a fantasy and the autumn fall would pass without her. Fighting

the tears that blurred her vision she
realised how much she hated leaving
the place she'd grown to love.

* * *

Next day her plans were upset when her
car broke down. It had been difficult to
start for the last few days and this time
appeared to have given up completely.

'Why go?' Laura was unconcerned.
'Stay until Richard comes home and let
him deal with your car.' She studied the
strain on Annie's face and the dark
circles under her eyes. 'Anyway a few
more days won't matter and you
deserve a rest after your hard work.'

'I must get back,' her voice broke and
then steadied. 'Even if I go on the train.
Is there a local garage that would look
at my car?' The very idea of meeting
Richard again was out of the question
especially as she knew he'd been with
Pascale.

'Well, of course, if you insist then you
must go but I shall miss you dear.'

Laura's eyes were shadowed. 'I do wish you'd wait until Richard comes before you leave. I'm sure he'll want to see you.'

'There's absolutely no need,' she told her gently. 'Everyone is familiar with the new system and it's running smoothly. Honestly Laura I wouldn't be going unless I knew everything was all right this end.'

'Well, if you feel you must,' the older woman repeated, 'but surely you don't want to take your luggage and books on the train.'

'I've got to get there somehow,' she said firmly. 'I'm running a business,' then smiling at Laura added, 'I know it's only tiny but I've already left it for longer than usual and I really do need to see for myself what's happening. Also I must get on to the next job, I'm only a beginner in the business world but even I see that I've got to keep the money rolling in.'

'Well, it's obvious really, isn't it?

'Sorry?'

'I'll drive you of course, I don't know why I didn't think of it before.'

Oh no, thought Annie, she couldn't allow that. Richard would think she had taken advantage of his mother's kind nature. 'No Laura, I couldn't allow you to do that. But if you could run me to the station . . . '

Laura seemed resigned to her decision then just as they were leaving they bumped into Steve coming to collect some papers. Quickly she took the opportunity to describe Annie's problem and just as quickly Steve offered to drive her home.

'It's far too far,' Annie protested

'Rubbish. We'll leave now and I can make my way back later during the day. Unless,' he added slyly, 'you've a spare bed.'

'You haven't seen my flat,' she retorted, 'it's not exactly a stately home, you could describe it as being on the small side.'

'Okay,' he grinned, 'I get the message. I can work in a visit to a client so you don't have to look so guilty.'

'Such a nice man,' Laura murmured. 'I hope you didn't mind me telling him about your problem I guessed he would help as Richard isn't here.'

'You're wonderful Laura.' She laughed. 'From buying bikinis to arranging transport home, you deal with it all.'

'I think it's part of being a mother. You never really get out of the habit of coping with problems. You'll know what I mean one day when you've children of your own.'

Dear Laura, life was so simple and clear cut for her. What would she say if she knew about the stormy relationship she'd had with her son? Perhaps she wouldn't be so keen to have her stay longer but probably even that would also be solved in the same matter of fact way.

'I'm sure you'll come back, one day.' Laura kissed her warmly.

'Perhaps,' she answered knowing she would never return.

The journey home, though longer

than anticipated, was relaxed and easy with Steve being his usual friendly self. At one point she took the opportunity to ask about the old couple and their shop on the Isle of Wight. Steve laughed good naturedly. 'You've got completely the wrong idea. He was bidding against Pascale's father and making sure the old couple could stay on if they wished.'

Oh dear, was she always going to misjudge him? She settled down to her own thoughts. When they reached her apartment, Steve made no demands and as he was running short of time for his appointment, did not even come in. As grateful as she was for the lift, she waved him off with a sense of relief.

After that it was surprising how easy it was to slip back into the old routine. If only she could deal with her emotions in the same way. Then, thankfully, after a couple of days she was able to plunge into work with a job that had come in while she was away. The new job took care of the days as she forced her mind to concentrate but there were still the evenings and worst of all the nights.

Her flat seemed incredibly tiny after the spacious luxury of Richard's house and London was hot and dusty. Time after time, her mind turned to the coolness of the forest and the beauty of the old thatched house with its pool and sprawling gardens.

She was worried that there had been no word from Steve about her car and a couple of times had started to dial his number but changed her mind. The new job was on a bus route and as much as she wanted her old car with her, was reluctant to communicate with even Steve. Her emotions were too raw and the pain too new to make contact with anyone in the Forest an easy option. Anyway she was confident Steve or the garage would ring her when the necessary work was completed. Of course, once she knew it was ready there would then be the ordeal of finding a way to collect it. As long as it stayed at the garage for collection she might be able to go there and back without anyone knowing she was in the area.

It delighted her to have a note from Katie telling her she was right and she and Lucy were very best friends again. What a thoughtful child she was once you managed to get through to her. Annie wrote an affectionate little note of thanks to Laura for looking after her so well. She'd grown fond of the older woman and it would have been nice to keep in touch but of course that was out of the question. There was Richard. Always there was Richard.

* * *

The call came the second week she was home. While going through her morning post, the telephone rang and with her mind still on the letter she was reading, she reached for the receiver. Before she'd even finished giving her name she was interrupted, 'Annie?' It slid through her fingers and clattered to the desk and then forcing herself to take deep breaths she grasped it firmly and held it to her ear.

'What the hell's going on, Annie are you there?' Evidently the caller was still speaking, his voice becoming so loud that she held the receiver slightly away from her ear.

Forcing the words out through chattering teeth, she replied, 'Richard, what do you want?'

'You've got to get back here,' he yelled.

Once more the receiver threatened to slip from her grasp, then she tightened her hold. 'Oh no, my job's finished.'

'You don't understand, something's gone wrong,' he told her sharply.

'Laura,' she gasped, 'is Laura all right and Katie?'

'What?' he sounded confused. 'Of course Mother's all right, she's gone to her bungalow and there's nothing wrong with Katie.'

'What do you want Richard?'

'Something's wrong at the office.' He

hesitated. 'The new system, it's not working at all well. You'll have to sort it out.'

'Not working, are you sure?'

'You heard what I said.' He sounded at the end of his patience. 'Be on the 9.15 tomorrow, I'll meet you at the station.'

'I most certainly will not, I . . . ' The line was dead. Richard had hung up.

Damn the arrogant man, she certainly would not be on the train tomorrow. How dare he assume she could drop everything and come running. Her system couldn't be wrong, it just couldn't. She'd checked and tested everything. If anything was amiss it was in the operation but even there she'd made certain everyone knew what they were doing. There was no way, absolutely no way she would go running at his bidding. But a little voice told her it wouldn't be good if a problem got back to Gallings.

Her eyes were drawn to him as the train drew in and she knew she would never get over her love for this man. The sun shone on his fair hair, high-lighting it with gold. Tall and straight in jeans and a casual shirt he looked both irritable and impatient. Nervously she ran her hands down the legs of her own jeans and tucking in her silk blouse wondered if she was too casually dressed.

He was pacing the platform as the train finally slowed and stepping down she tried to read something in his face. Then licking her dry lips she started to greet him but he barely spoke, brusquely grabbing her arm and hustling her into the parked car.

'What the hell is going on?' she said indignantly, rubbing the top of her arm where his fingers had dug in.

'I'll explain at the house,' he said briefly and lapsed into silence.

It had better be good, she fumed determinedly staring straight ahead. If he thinks I'm staying here for a few more weeks, he's got another think coming and I shall tell him so. Nothing would induce me to stay here ever again. And, resolving to hear him out, give her opinion and then be on her way, Annie sunk into the familiar luxury of the upholstery.

The journey was brief and soon they were swinging into the drive. Quickly she opened her door not wanting to feel his hands on her again. One look at his amused face caused her to flush as she realised he knew what she was thinking. Then he was propelling her quickly along the path towards the white-washed brick and timbered house.

Listening to the door slam behind them she whirled around angrily to face him. 'This had better be good. I've done my job properly and frankly I'm too busy to do a hand holding operation for your staff,' she fumed at him.

'Staff?' He looked blank.

'Isn't that the reason I'm here, because they don't understand the system?'

He smiled sheepishly. 'The system is

working perfectly.'

'What?' she practically screamed.

'Brilliant, you did a brilliant job.'

'Then why did you make me drop everything and rush down here?'

He didn't answer.

'Richard,' she said slowly. 'Why exactly am I here? I really thought you'd given Gallings a bad report and well, I might as well admit it. I rely on them.'

He ignored her comments. 'I . . . em . . . I've got a cheque for the work you did. Here,' he picked up an envelope from the table and handed it to her.

She took the envelope. 'You could have posted it. What is going on?'

'Oh, and as a little bonus your car has been repaired and re-sprayed. The garage found a number of little jobs to do on it.'

'Thank you,' she flushed, feeling rather embarrassed. 'That's very kind of you. Is it ready?'

'Oh yes, it's in my garage.'

'Fine,' she turned away. 'If you'd get

it out for me, I'll be on my way.'

'No.'

'What do you mean, no?' Nervously she clasped her hands together. 'Is there something else?'

She met his eyes and it was difficult to look away. 'Richard what is it?'

'I want you to marry me.' It was said so softly that it took a few moments for the words to register.

'What did you say?'

He stood quite still as though frightened to touch her. 'I want you to marry me.'

Annie looked for somewhere to sit down and subsided on the second stair. Kneeling on the stair below he placed a hand on either side of her face and whispered, 'Look I'm on my knees, what more can I do?' His thumbs stroked the corners of her mouth. 'I can't live without you.'

'You . . . you can't?' she gulped.

'Definitely not. I never wanted you to leave, you know that.'

Somehow she was in his arms with

his mouth warm and demanding on her lips. 'You only wanted me to live with you . . . ' She tried to speak in between kisses. 'You didn't say you wanted to marry me.'

'I didn't think it through. I assumed just to have you living with me would be enough but I came back and Mother said you'd gone off with Steve.'

'Steve?' she interrupted, 'but he only gave me a lift home.'

'I know that now but Mother let me think you'd gone off together. I reckon she knew how I felt and tried to make me admit it to myself. Well anyway, I saw red and could have cheerfully killed Steve. I knew then that I wanted you to belong to me in every sense. I needed the security of knowing you were my wife.'

The words were wrung from him and she realised how much it cost this strong and self-sufficient man to tell her what she longed to hear.

'And do you really love me?' Suddenly she had him in her power.

'Annie I adore you. I think I must have loved you from the first moment I set eyes on you.' He paused at her look of disbelief. 'Even if I didn't realise it immediately, I knew that you affected me like no other woman I'd ever met.'

'I would never have guessed. You were terribly rude and everything I said seemed to be wrong.'

'You were lovely, like a small kitten trying its strength by spitting at everybody.' He took the slide from her hair. 'I couldn't resist fighting with you although most of the time I think I was fighting myself. You were becoming far too important in my life.'

'You were getting to be important to me as well.'

He laughed gently. 'There was I thinking that you only liked accountants.'

'What on earth gave you that idea?'

'Why you did of course,' he said indignantly. 'First there was Mark and then Steve. You all seemed to speak the same language.'

'And I thought you went for the femme fatale type of woman. In any case Steve told me you were very much against blondes. Then I heard you were in France the same time as Pascale.'

'What?' He watched her face and then enlightenment dawned. 'Oh you think we were over there together do you? I believe you're jealous.'

'Of course I'm not,' she answered indignantly, 'but you must admit it's a bit of a coincidence. I know you'd told me it was all finished but she gave me the impression you were meeting there.'

'Maybe, but France is a big country and she goes regularly to Paris to see her relations, while I was working in Brittany.'

'I see,' was all she said and wondered why she'd ever doubted him.

'What about Steve? Even that time I telephoned, you wouldn't speak to me because you were going out with Steve.'

'Only because I was so miserable, besides Steve had already guessed how I felt about you.'

Later when she could get her breath back she continued. 'You were telling me about the first time you saw me,' she smiled. 'Did you know you were going to love me?'

'I knew that very first time. I saw a beautiful and clever young woman and I knew that with you in my home I'd have a better chance to prise you out from your shell.' His hands were roaming her face and neck and stroking her hair. 'But the ice was thick, far thicker than I thought, and I had to chip away at it day by day.'

She was silent as his deep voice crooned everything she wanted to hear.

'Sometimes I worried in case I had really hurt you badly but I wanted you to love and need to be loved, by me.'

'I've loved you for a long time,' she told him truthfully as the revelation of just how long, came to her.

'Sometimes,' he continued, 'I felt I was winning and then just at the last minute the barriers would come up. My biggest fault was I underestimated your independence and was stupid enough to suggest you work for me. Can you forgive me? I was a fool because it's that independence, coupled with everything else about you, that's so devastating.'

'Oh,' she teased, 'just as I thought, you only loved me for my body.'

'I love you every way there is,' he answered seriously. 'Besides I want a woman in my life who I can discuss business with, not as you thought, some little thing without a brain. The woman I want in my life is clever and beautiful. Everything I need is packed in that one person: you.'

She licked her lips. 'And how long are you likely to want this woman?'

He looked at her as though she was speaking another language. 'Why forever of course. Aren't I asking you to marry me?'

'Then ask properly,' she pulled away from him.

'You don't mean the one knee stuff.'

'No silly, just ask me.'

'Will you marry me darling?'

'Yes,' she breathed, 'oh yes.' She hesitated for only a moment. 'Katie?' she asked at the same time crossing her fingers.

'Katie's delighted.'

'She knows?' She narrowed her eyes at him.

He grinned. 'I told her I was going to ask you and she said something about you understanding girls. I think she meant that I didn't.'

It was much later that they began to talk.

'There's just this one little problem,' he nibbled her earlobe. 'Em . . . where shall we live?'

She decided to call his bluff. 'Why London of course, in my apartment.' She looked around the large sunny room and, turning wide innocent eyes to him, added, 'Of course it's a little on the small side,' teasingly.

'If you want to live in London I suppose we could work something out. He was obviously not liking the idea but carried on, 'I could buy a flat and perhaps we could share our time between the two places.'

She kissed the tip of his nose but said nothing, just waited for the explosion that was coming.

'Honestly though Annie, as much as I love you, my business is chandlery and I can hardly carry that on in the middle of town.' He hesitated, 'But on the other hand . . . '

She was instantly suspicious. 'Yes?'

'I . . . em . . . made a few enquiries and there's a very nice little office in Southampton.' He looked a little sheepish. 'At the risk of a lecture on women's rights I wondered if you could move your business there. I know you wouldn't like to give it up altogether,' he said wistfully.

'I see,' she said. 'I'm to move my business while yours stays where it is.'

'Em . . . yes.'

'That's the only sensible solution.'

'What? Am I hearing things?' He shook his head.

'I can hardly keep you on what I earn,' she said slyly. 'So you will just have to keep your business going. But on the other hand you could keep me very nicely if I gave mine up.'

He hugged her to him. 'You're being very amenable. I think I'm going to miss our fights.'

'Oh, I know when to play the little woman,' she laughed. 'But I expect we shall still fight. Perhaps not so much if you're running your business and I'm running mine.'

'Would you give it up?' he said hopefully.

'Absolutely not.'

'Not ever?'

'Well maybe one day and then you can be the only breadwinner but until then it's an equal partnership. Agreed?'

'Agreed,' he sighed, kissing her again. 'Let's go and get Katie and tell her our good news.'

We do hope that you have enjoyed reading this large print book.

Did you know that all of our titles are available for purchase?

We publish a wide range of high quality large print books including:
Romances, Mysteries, Classics
General Fiction
Non Fiction and Westerns

Special interest titles available in large print are:
The Little Oxford Dictionary
Music Book, Song Book
Hymn Book, Service Book

Also available from us courtesy of Oxford University Press:
Young Readers' Dictionary
(large print edition)
Young Readers' Thesaurus
(large print edition)

For further information or a free brochure, please contact us at:
Ulverscroft Large Print Books Ltd.,
The Green, Bradgate Road, Anstey,
Leicester, LE7 7FU, England.
Tel: (00 44) **0116 236 4325**
Fax: (00 44) **0116 234 0205**

TROPICAL NIGHTS

Phyllis Humphrey

Tracy Barnes has a few words for real-estate mogul Gregory Thompson. Infuriating. Obstinate. Presumptuous. He's bought the Hawaiian hotel where she works as assistant manager and she could be forced out of her job. If it wasn't for his charm she'd hate him. But Gregory, confident in his ability to win over the guarded Tracy, plans dinner, dancing, and a moonlit walk. Maybe it's Hawaii, but Gregory hasn't felt this good in years . . . or wanted a woman this badly . . .